Waiting for Bad News!

I rolled onto my back and Dee Dee started to scratch my tummy.

"You know, there's one thing I don't understand about Adam," I said.

"What's that?" Dee Dee asked.

"He knows I can talk," I said. "He made me talk in the basement of the yacht club before you and the policeman saved me."

"But he couldn't prove it," Dee Dee said.

"I know, but he doesn't even act like he remembers," I said.

"It's a good point," Dee Dee said. "We'd better stay on guard around him."

Look for:

Wordsworth and the . . .

Cold Cut Catastrophe
Kibble Kidnapping
Roast Beef Romance
Mail-Order Meatloaf Mess
Tasty Treat Trick
Lip-Smacking Licorice Love Affair°

From HarperPaperbacks

° coming soon

Wordsworth and the Tasty Treat Trick

by Todd Strasser

HarperPaperbacks
A Division of HarperCollinsPublishers

This is a work of fiction. The characters, incidents, and dialogues are products of the author's imagination and are not to be construed as real. Any resemblance to actual events or persons, living or dead, is entirely coincidental.

HarperPaperbacks *A Division of* HarperCollins*Publishers*
10 East 53rd Street, New York, N.Y. 10022

Cover and interior illustrations by Leif Peng
Cover and interior art ©1996 Creative Media Applications, Inc.

First printing: February 1996

Printed in the United States of America

HarperPaperbacks and colophon are trademarks of HarperCollins*Publishers*

❖ 10 9 8 7 6 5 4 3 2 1

For the Kreegers

Clip!

"Ow! Oooch! Yikes!" I, Maxwell Short Wordsworth the Sixth, was writhing in pain. "Stop! You're cutting off parts of my body!"

"Give me a break, Wordsworth," said my best friend and tormentor, Dee Dee Chandler.

Clip!

"Aaaah! Oh, no! Yeow!" I cried out in miserable agony.

"You're such a crybaby," Dee Dee teased good-naturedly. "I'm only clipping the very tips of your nails."

"But I have extremely sensitive nail tips!" I cried. "It hurts!"

"No, it doesn't. I even called Dr. Hopka and asked him if cutting nails hurts. He said it's all in your head."

Dr. Hopka is my veterinarian and a nationally known sadist. I'm sure he's wanted by the FBI and the ASPCA for cruelty to animals.

Clip!

"Yeooowch!" I wailed. By the way, did I mention that I'm a basset hound? Well, I am, and in case you haven't noticed, I talk. But only Dee Dee knows that. She is ten years old and has blond hair and freckles. She can talk to me anytime she wants, but I can talk to her only when the rest of the Chandler family isn't around.

Ding dong! The front doorbell rang.

"Who could that be?" Dee Dee asked. "We're not expecting anyone."

Maybe it was the ASPCBH, the American Society for the Prevention of Cruelty to Basset Hounds. They had come to arrest her.

Dee Dee went down the hall to the front door. I followed a safe distance behind, in case it was a dangerous stranger.

Through the narrow window beside the front door I saw a boy's face. He looked vaguely familiar, but I couldn't quite remember where I'd seen him before. Neither could Dee Dee.

"Who are you?" she asked.

"Adam," the boy said.

"Who?" Dee Dee frowned.

"Adam Pickney, your next-door neighbor."

Dee Dee and I stared through the narrow window in disbelief. Could it be true? The last time we'd seen Adam, he'd had long black hair, several earrings, and a nose ring. He'd been wearing a black shirt, black jeans, and boots. The boy we were looking at now had short, neatly combed black hair. He was wearing a light blue oxford shirt, tucked into plaid shorts. He wore white tennis shoes and long white socks that ended just below his knees. His skin was pale, as if he hadn't been out in the sun in a long time.

If clothes could speak, his would have said "geek."

Dee Dee opened the narrow glass window. "Is that really you, Adam?"

"Hard to believe, huh?" Adam asked with a self-conscious smile.

"I'll say," Dee Dee said. "So what do you want?"

"Nothing," he said. "I just came over to say hi."

Dee Dee glanced down at me with a scowl. The Chandlers have lived next to the Pickneys for a long time, but Adam has never come over to our house before. He used to say he hated the Chandlers. The last time we saw him was when he kidnapped me and tried to get me to talk so that he could make a video-tape of me and sell it for a fortune. But Dee Dee saved me, and the police came and took Adam away.

"That's all, just to say hi?" Dee Dee asked skeptically.

Wordsworth and the Tasty Treat Trick

"Well, not really," Adam admitted sheepishly. "I guess I also wanted to say that I'm sorry about kidnapping Wordsworth. I mean, it was pretty dumb of me."

Dee Dee nodded uncertainly. Was Adam actually apologizing? This was very, *very* strange.

"I guess I've really learned a lot since then," Adam said. After Adam kidnapped me, the police discovered that he and his friend Joseph had been breaking into cars and stealing radios and CD players. After that, Mr. Pickney, Adam's father and the mayor of Soundview Manor, had sent him away somewhere.

"What did you learn?" Dee Dee asked.

"Well, you know." Adam gave her a slightly embarrassed smile. "Like not to be the kind of dirtbag person I used to be."

Just then the Chandlers' big old car pulled into the driveway in front of the house. Leyland Chandler, Dee Dee's father, got out. He is a tall thin man with white hair. He pressed his hands into the small of his back and stretched.

"Ah, that's better," he groaned with pleasure. Then he went around to the trunk of the car and opened it. Inside was a large device that looked like a vacuum cleaner with wheels and a seat attached to it. Leyland started to pull the device out of the trunk. His face turned red as he strained under its weight.

"Wait, Mr. Chandler, let me help!" Adam hurried across the porch and down the front steps. He joined Leyland behind the car and helped him lift the device out of the car's trunk.

Dee Dee looked down at me with surprise on her face. "Do you believe it?" she whispered. "Adam helping Dad?"

"Maybe it's a trick," I whispered back.

Together, Adam and Mr. Chandler carried the device up the front steps. Dee Dee opened the front door and they carried it inside and put it down in the hall.

"Thank you very much," Leyland said, dusting off his hands. "It's rather heavy. I'm not sure I could have gotten it up the steps alone."

"What is it?" Adam asked.

"My latest invention," Leyland said proudly. "The Chandler E-Z Glide Self-Propelled Riding Vacuum Cleaner."

"You mean, you ride it like one of those lawn mowers for people who have big lawns?" Adam asked.

"Yes, precisely," Leyland said. "Except this is for people with large houses to vacuum."

"What a great idea!" Adam said.

"Why, thank you." Leyland beamed. "I'm rather proud of it myself."

"You've made a lot of other inventions, haven't you?" Adam asked.

"Why, yes, hundreds," Dee Dee's father replied.

"Wow." Adam shook his head. "I can't believe I've been living right next to you all these years and I never came over to see what you were doing."

"You've been living next door to us?" Leyland scratched his head and gave Adam a puzzled look. "That's odd. I don't recall ever seeing you before."

"Dad, this is Adam Pickney," Dee Dee said.

Leyland's eyebrows rose with surprise. "Adam?"

"She's right, Mr. Chandler, it's me," Adam said.

"But you've changed," Leyland said.

"Yeah, I know." Adam nodded.

Just then I heard the sound of rapid footsteps as someone ran up the front steps. A moment later Dee Dee's big sister, Janine, dashed into the house and slammed the door behind her. She was breathing hard and pressed her back against the door. Her white tennis clothes were damp with sweat and her white socks were stained with red clay. That meant she'd been playing tennis.

"Made it!" she gasped. Then she slowly focused on Leyland, Dee Dee, myself, and finally . . . Adam.

"Ahhhhh!" she suddenly screamed, and jumped behind her father. "Keep him away from me!"

2

"Keep who away from you?" Mr. Chandler asked.

"Him!" Janine pointed a finger at Adam.

"Why?" asked Dee Dee.

"Because he's one of them," Janine cried.

"One of who?" asked Leyland.

"One of the guys who wants to take me to the sailing dance at the club," Janine said. "At least fifteen guys asked me today. They waited around the tennis courts, they trailed me to the snack bar. One of them just followed me home. They're driving me crazy!"

Janine is sixteen, blond, and strikingly beautiful by human standards. She is quite athletic, and has absolutely no use for boys.

"There's a dance at the club?" Adam asked.

"Oh, don't pretend you don't know," Janine said

angrily. Then she squinted at him. "Who are you, anyway? And where did you get those nerdy clothes?"

"It's Adam," Dee Dee said.

"Adam who?" Janine asked.

"Adam Pickney from next door," said Dee Dee.

Janine's jaw dropped. "Adam?"

"I've changed," Adam said.

Janine looked at her father. "Is this some kind of joke?"

"No, it's really me," Adam said. "Remember you poured perfume on my head when you caught me in the tree outside your bedroom?"

Janine nodded. "You look so different. What happened to you?"

"I learned my lesson," Adam said.

"Looks more like you had a frontal lobotomy," said Janine. "Who picked out that lame wardrobe?"

"Now, Janine," Leyland interrupted. "Clothes are a matter of individual taste. It's rude to make personal remarks."

"It's okay, Mr. Chandler," Adam said. "One of the things I learned while I was away is that wearing cool clothes is just another form of peer pressure. I've learned that you have to pick your own styles and find your own way in life. The most important thing is to be who you really are."

"Does that mean you're really a nerd?" Dee Dee asked innocently.

Adam grinned. "I hope not."

Janine blinked. "Wow, Adam, you really have changed."

Ding! Dong! The doorbell rang again. Janine quickly ran into the living room and hid.

"Tell whoever it is that I'm not here," she called.

Leyland opened the door. Outside stood a guy wearing a white T-shirt, jeans, and a green baseball cap.

"Can I help you?" Leyland asked.

The guy took off his cap. He had a blond crew cut, a ruggedly handsome face, and a muscular build. "Uh, hi, is this Janine Chandler's house?"

"Why, yes, it is."

"Is she around?" the guy asked.

"Not at the moment," Leyland said.

"Uh, think I could wait on the porch until she comes home?" the guy asked.

"Well, er . . ." Leyland clearly didn't know what to say.

"You can wait if you want," Adam said, "but she went to the city and probably won't be back until really late tonight. She may even stay at a friend's house and not come back until tomorrow."

"Oh." The guy looked disappointed. "Well, in

that case, would you just tell her Chuck came by, and not to tell any other guy she'll go to the dance with him until she talks to me?"

"Certainly," Leyland said.

"Thanks." Chuck left and Leyland closed the front door. Janine came out of the living room.

"Who's Chuck?" Dee Dee asked her.

"Just some guy who belongs to the yacht club," Janine said.

"He sure is good-looking," Dee Dee said.

"I don't even know him," said Janine, clearly perplexed. "I've never said two words to him in my life."

"Then why is he so eager to get you to go with him to the dance?" Leyland asked.

Janine sighed. "Believe me, Dad, I wish I knew."

3

Adam helped Leyland carry the Chandler E-Z Glide Self-Propelled Riding Vacuum Cleaner down to the workshop in the basement. Janine went upstairs to take a shower, and I went back to the kitchen. All the excitement had tired me out. It was time for a nice long nap in the sun.

It wasn't the most restful nap. It seemed like every five minutes the phone rang. When I finally got up, it was dinnertime. I stretched and yawned. Dee Dee was kneeling over me. She was wearing a bright red sweatshirt.

"Did you have a nice nap?" she asked, stroking my head affectionately.

"It was okay," I said. "Did the phone ring a lot or did I dream that?"

"The phone rang a lot," Dee Dee said. "All these boys are calling Janine about the dance."

"That's strange," I said. "Think you could give me a quick tummy scratch?"

"Of course."

I rolled onto my back and Dee Dee started to scratch my tummy.

"You know, there's one thing I don't understand about Adam," I said.

"What's that?" Dee Dee asked.

"He knows I can talk," I said. "He made me talk in the basement of the yacht club before you and the policeman saved me."

"But he couldn't prove it," Dee Dee said.

"I know, but he doesn't even act like he remembers," I said.

"It's a good point," Dee Dee said. "We better stay on guard around him. So, are you ready for dinner?"

"I guess." The thought of food no longer excited me the way it once had. I'd been put on a diet and had lost nearly twenty pounds. Thanks to the evil Dr. Hopka, my days of lamb chops and table scraps were over. Now I was forced to eat . . . dog food. Just the thought of it sent cold shivers through me.

"I know you don't like what we give you," Dee Dee said, standing up. "But you have to admit that you're much healthier now than you used to be."

"I'd like to see *you* go on a diet," I muttered. "Then I'd—"

"Shush!" Dee Dee held her finger to her lips. "Someone's coming."

A moment later Roy came in. He's Dee Dee's fourteen-year-old brother. He has brown hair, freckles, and braces. He looked around the kitchen and frowned.

"Were you just talking to someone?" he asked Dee Dee.

"Uh, no." Dee Dee shook her head innocently.

"That's weird," Roy said. "I could have sworn I heard someone else's voice."

He focused on his sister again. "Hey, isn't that Janine's sweatshirt?"

Dee Dee bit her lip.

"You better put it back," Roy said. "You know how she hates it when you wear her things."

"I'll put it back just as soon as I eat dinner," Dee Dee said.

"That reminds me," said Roy. "Guess who's eating with us tonight?"

"Who?" asked Dee Dee.

"Adam."

"Why?"

"I don't know." Roy shrugged. "He and Dad have been in the workshop all afternoon. So Dad asked him if he wanted to stay for dinner and he said yes."

"This is very weird," Dee Dee said. "Does Adam know what our dinners are like?"

Wordsworth and the Tasty Treat Trick

"I doubt it," said Roy. "But I guess he's going to find out."

Brrriiinggggg! The phone started to ring.

"Are you going to answer it?" Dee Dee asked.

"Let the phone machine get it," Roy said. "It's just another guy calling Janine." He went over to the kitchen counter and took out the bread. Almost every night at dinner Roy had a triple-decker peanut-butter-and-jelly sandwich. Meanwhile Dee Dee poured some dog food into my bowl. I gave her the saddest look possible. Why couldn't I have a lamb chop, just this once?

"Don't give me that look," she said. As I said before, Dee Dee often talks to me in front of other people. I just have to make sure I don't talk back.

"Oh, and listen, I heard something cool on TV," Roy said as he spread peanut butter on the bread. The scent of that peanut butter made my stomach grumble with longing.

"What?" Dee Dee asked.

"The ASHV van is coming to Soundview Manor."

"What's ASHV?" Dee Dee asked.

"'America's Stupidest Home Videos,'" Roy explained. "They have vans that go all around the country making videos of the stupid things people do. They also collect videos other people have made."

Forget dog food. The smell of that peanut butter

was driving me mad. Neither Dee Dee nor Roy was paying attention to me. I crept across the floor toward the kitchen counter.

"Oh, right," Dee Dee said. "They're always showing videos of people either falling off things or crashing into things. They're always falling off docks and trees, and they're always crashing their bikes into bushes and fences. It's really dumb."

"Well, I think it would be really cool to get a video on the show," Roy said.

"But don't they have to take a video of you doing something stupid?"

"Not always," Roy said. "A lot of the videos they show are homemade. And a lot of them are just stunts made to look like accidents."

I stopped at Roy's feet. The kitchen counter was just above my head. Now that I was a svelte seventy-five pounds, I was certain I could jump up and grab the sandwich with my teeth.

"So you're going to fake doing something really stupid just to get your video on the show?" Dee Dee asked.

"You got it." Roy had finished spreading the jelly. The sandwich sat on a plate on the counter.

"But we don't have a video camera," Dee Dee said.

"I know, that's a problem," Roy said as he opened the refrigerator to get out the milk.

Wordsworth and the Tasty Treat Trick

This was my chance. I knew Dee Dee would be furious with me, but I couldn't help myself. I was a dog who'd been raised on fine meats! Dee Dee didn't understand what it was like to have to eat dog food day after day. It was torture!

I jumped up and grabbed the sandwich with my mouth.

"Wordsworth!" Dee Dee shouted.

I started to run. I had to get out of the kitchen and find a place where I could eat without being disturbed.

"Hey! Come back here!" Roy shouted. He and Dee Dee started to chase me. I raced out of the kitchen and headed down the hall. Suddenly two hands came out of nowhere and grabbed my collar. "Not so fast, big guy."

4

I looked up to see who'd caught me. It was Adam!

"I know how you must feel, Wordsworth," he said sympathetically as he pulled Roy's peanut-butter-and-jelly sandwich out of my mouth. "But this isn't good for you. Here, try one of these instead."

To my amazement, Adam reached into his pocket, took out a dog biscuit, and fed it to me. Hey, it tasted pretty good!

Woof! Woof! I quickly barked for another one.

"You can have another one, Wordsworth," he said, "*after* you eat your dinner."

Well, in that case . . . I hurried back past Roy and Dee Dee and into the kitchen, where I stuck my snout into that dog food and started to eat.

"What'd you give him?" I heard Dee Dee ask Adam.

"One of these organic dog biscuits," Adam said. "They're made out of soybeans with all natural ingredients and flavorings. They've got no fat and hardly any calories. I told him he could have another after he finished his dinner."

Woof! Woof! I finished my yucky dog food and barked eagerly for another of those delicious biscuits.

"Here you go." Adam tossed me one and I quickly gobbled it up. Soybeans or no soybeans, it was a definite yum!

"How come you brought dog biscuits?" Dee Dee asked Adam.

"Well, when I came over to tell you I was sorry about kidnapping Wordsworth, I wanted to show him I was sorry, too," Adam explained.

The rest of the Chandlers started to come into the kitchen, including Flora, Dee Dee's mom. She's an artist who always wears white clothes and has long blond hair. Like everyone else in the Chandler family that day, she was very surprised to find Adam with short hair, an oxford shirt, and plaid shorts.

"Adam Pickney?" Her eyes widened slightly.

"It's me, Mrs. Chandler," Adam said.

"You've changed," said Dee Dee's mother.

"That's what I keep telling everyone," Adam said.

"Adam and I worked all afternoon on the Chandler E-Z Glide Self-Propelled Riding Vacuum

Cleaner," Leyland said. "He proved himself to be a willing and able assistant, so I invited him to stay for dinner."

Frankly, I didn't see what the big deal was. Dinner at the Chandler house simply meant that everyone fended for themselves and then sat together while they ate. Flora usually had a salad. Leyland had cold soup. Janine often bought a sub at the sandwich shop in town. Roy had his peanut-butter-and-jelly sandwich, and Dee Dee had breakfast cereal.

Janine came in. She immediately glared at her little sister. "Dee Dee, what have I told you about taking my things without asking?"

"But every time I ask, you say no," Dee Dee said.

"Oh, I get it," Janine said. "So since I always say no, you figured, why bother to ask?"

Dee Dee nodded.

"I'll count to three, and if you don't have that off, I'm going to take it off you right in front of Adam," Janine threatened.

Dee Dee ran up to her room to change. Janine turned back to the kitchen table. "Darn," she said, "I was in such a rush to get home that I forgot to buy a sub."

"Don't worry," Adam said. "I'll cook something."

Everyone stared at him in amazement. Adam Pickney was going to cook for the Chandlers?

5

———— ∞∞ ————

Roy and Janine gave each other shocked looks.

"Did he say *cook*?" Roy asked. "That's a word I haven't heard in this house in years."

"It's a very nice offer, Adam," said Janine. "But I don't think you'll find much to work with in this kitchen."

"On the contrary," Adam said as he pulled open the refrigerator door. "I see milk, bread, and eggs. That's all I need to make French toast."

"French toast for dinner?" Flora asked, delighted. "What a splendid idea!"

Soon the kitchen was filled with the smell of sizzling French toast.

"Is something burning?" Dee Dee cried as she hurried back into the kitchen, wearing one of her own sweatshirts.

Wordsworth and the Tasty Treat Trick

"No, darling," Flora said. "Adam's cooking."

"Adam? Cooking?" Dee Dee looked shocked.

Adam wound up making enough for everyone. Then he joined them at the kitchen table and ate.

"Wow, this is really good," Roy said. "Can you teach me how to cook French toast?"

"Sure," Adam said. "It's easy."

Ding! Dong! The sound of the doorbell echoed down the hall to the kitchen.

Flora frowned. "Who could that be?"

"It's probably another guy who wants to take me to the sailing dance," Janine groaned.

"I thought that dance wasn't scheduled for another month," Leyland said.

"It's not," said Janine.

"Maybe it would be easier if you just said yes," Dee Dee suggested.

"But I don't want to go," Janine said. "Especially with one of those guys who's always hanging around the yacht club. They've all got such dumb, macho attitudes toward women."

Ding! Dong! The doorbell rang again.

"I really wish they wouldn't disturb us at dinner," Leyland said.

"I'll take care of it." Adam got up and went down the hall to the front door.

As soon as he was out of earshot, Flora turned to

23

LINDA S. SEYBOLD LIBRARY
FERN HILL ELEMENTARY SCHOOL
915 LINCOLN AVENUE
WEST CHESTER, PA 19380-4583

the rest of the family. "Are you *sure* that's Adam Pickney?"

"Hard to believe, isn't it?" Janine said in a low voice.

"If you look close, there's a definite resemblance," said Dee Dee. "And you can see the little holes in his ear where the earrings used to be."

"He certainly has changed for the better," Leyland said. "He was immensely helpful down in the workshop. He even said he'd like to be my apprentice."

"Oh, Leyland, darling, that's wonderful!" Flora clasped her hands happily. "You always said you wanted an apprentice."

Meanwhile Adam's voice echoed down the hallway. "No, I'm sorry, but she doesn't want to speak to anyone right now. . . . Well, that's too bad. Why don't you just leave her alone?"

Bang! The door slammed. A moment later Adam returned to the kitchen.

"Sorry about slamming the door," he apologized. "Some people just can't take no for an answer."

"Thanks, Adam, I really appreciate it," Janine said. "I just don't understand why they're all so intent on taking me to the dance. Especially when they know I'm not interested."

"I know why," Roy said.

6

<hr />

Everyone stared at him.

"You know why all those guys are asking Janine to go to the dance?" Dee Dee asked.

"Sure," Roy said. "I was at the club yesterday and I overheard Chuck Reilly and Erik Blinder talking about it. Fifteen guys got together and bet twenty dollars each. The guy who gets Janine to go to the dance wins all the money."

"Three hundred dollars?" Janine gasped.

"That's right," Roy said.

"Make a deal with one of them!" Dee Dee told her big sister. "Tell him you'll go if he splits the money with you."

Groof! I barked in agreement. It was an excellent idea.

"Forget it, Dee Dee," Janine said. "There's no way I'm going with any of them. Especially now that I know there's a bet. That's the most disgusting thing I ever heard. It makes me feel like I'm a horse or something."

"Don't worry, darling." Leyland patted her on the shoulder. "You'd be a Thoroughbred, at least."

"Gee, thanks, Dad." Janine rolled her eyes.

Brrrriiiinnnnggg! The phone rang. Everyone stared at it.

"Don't bother answering it," Janine said.

"I do wish there was something you could do to make them stop," Flora said.

"I'm sorry, everyone," Janine said. "I know it's not fair that they keep bothering you. I just don't know what to do."

After dinner, Dee Dee took me for a walk in Soundview Manor Park. After I stopped to sniff a few dozen trees and bushes, we sat down on the rocks near Bell Island Sound. I put my head in Dee Dee's lap and she scratched me behind the ear.

"What a strange day," she said.

"I'm sorry about the peanut-butter-and-jelly sandwich," I said. "I couldn't help it. After weeks of that awful bland dog food, I just lost control."

"I understand." Dee Dee patted my head affectionately. "I should have given you a special treat once in a while. Those flavored soybean dog biscuits sound like just the thing."

"Why don't we skip the dog biscuits and just have filet mignon once a week?" I asked.

Dee Dee smirked. "Don't push your luck, Wordsworth."

We sat on the rocks and watched the sailboats glide across the sound. A white motorboat with a flashing blue light raced past.

"What's that?" I asked.

"The harbor police," Dee Dee said. "There must be a boat that's in trouble. Can you believe those boys got together and made that bet to see who could get Janine to go to the dance?"

"I can believe *that*," I said. "What I have a hard time believing is the change in Adam."

"I know," said Dee Dee. "That's really strange."

"Do you think he's faking?" I asked. "Or is it really real?"

"Who knows?" Dee Dee shrugged. "I mean, he looks so different. And coming over to apologize . . . That's so unlike the old Adam."

"And bringing me biscuits," I added.

"Right," Dee Dee said. "If the old Adam did that, I'd know he was up to no good. But now I have to wonder, what could he possibly want?"

"Maybe he doesn't want anything," I said. "Maybe

he really has changed and he's doing all these nice things to make up for when he was so mean."

Dee Dee leaned her chin against her knee. "Maybe, Wordsworth, but I just don't know."

7

In the weeks that followed, Adam spent more time at the Chandlers' house than he did at his own. Almost every day he came over and helped Leyland in the workshop. They were building a new improved version of the Chandler E-Z Glide Self-Propelled Riding Vacuum Cleaner. Sometimes at night Adam even cooked the family dinner. He never said anything about knowing I could talk, and he always brought a tasty treat for me when he came. I know it's hard to believe, but I actually started to look forward to his daily visits.

So did Roy.

"Where's Adam?" Roy asked one morning in the kitchen. He was standing by the kitchen window, peering over at the Pickneys' house.

"Why don't you sit down and eat some breakfast, darling," Flora said.

"Yeah, what's the big deal?" Dee Dee asked.

"I came up with the perfect stunt for 'America's Stupidest Home Videos,'" Roy said. "Adam said he'd bring over his video camera today and help me film it."

"What's the stunt?" Janine asked.

"It's a secret," Roy said. "But if you want to come down to the park in a little while, you can watch."

Ding! Dong! The front doorbell rang.

"Oh, no, not again!" Janine groaned. Hardly a day passed without several guys coming by and begging her to go to the club dance. The phones rang so often that Leyland had turned them off. As the day of the dance grew closer the boys seemed to come by more and more often.

"How much longer until this stops?" Flora asked.

"The dance is in three days," Roy said. "I guess it'll end after that."

Ding! Dong!

"Would someone please go tell whoever it is to go away?" Janine asked.

"I'll go," Dee Dee said. "Come on, Wordsworth."

I got up and followed her to the front door. Sometimes, lately, Janine's suitors were *too* persistent. If they wouldn't leave the door, Dee Dee encouraged me to bark menacingly at them. I sort of enjoyed it.

Dee Dee opened the narrow window beside the front door. "That's funny, there's no one . . . Oh, my gosh!"

The scent of a dozen of different flowers reached my nose as Dee Dee opened the front door. On the porch stood a beautiful bouquet!

"Oh, Janine!" Dee Dee cried, picking up the bouquet and hurrying back toward the kitchen. "Look what someone left for you!"

Dee Dee put the bouquet down on the kitchen table. "Isn't it beautiful?"

"Lovely," said Flora.

"Except that it must be from one of those guys who's trying to get me to go to the dance," Janine said woefully.

"Look!" Dee Dee pulled a small white envelope out of the flowers and handed it to her sister. "It has your name on it."

Janine shrugged and scooped up another spoonful of Cheerios.

"Aren't you going to read it?" Dee Dee wanted to know.

"What's the point?" Janine asked. "Whoever sent them did it because they want to win the money, not because they like me."

"Still, the least you can do is read the note," Dee Dee said.

"If you're so interested, why don't you read it?" Janine demanded.

"Okay." Dee Dee opened the envelope. She took out a small white card and read, "'Dearest Janine, Don't confuse me with the others. My feelings for you are sincere. Faithfully Yours, A Secret Admirer.'"

"Wow!" Dee Dee put the card down. "A secret admirer!"

Janine picked up the card and studied it. "Why wouldn't he put his name on it?"

"Maybe he's shy," Flora said.

"Believe me, Mom, those guys are anything but shy."

"Then maybe it's not from one of those guys," said Roy.

Tap! Tap! Someone tapped on the sliding glass door next to the kitchen. I looked up and saw Adam out on the deck carrying a video camera.

"Oh, great, he's here!" Roy jumped up and opened the sliding door.

Adam stepped in. "Hi, everyone."

Groof! Groof! I barked eagerly.

"Oh, yeah, here you go, Wordsworth." Adam tossed me a scrumptious treat, which I immediately gobbled up.

"Hey, Adam," Dee Dee said. "Look what Janine just got!"

Wordsworth and the Tasty Treat Trick

Adam looked at the flowers and smiled. "They're really nice." Then he turned to Roy. "Ready to go?"

"Don't you want to know who sent them?" Dee Dee asked.

"Uh . . ." Adam grinned nervously. "Yeah, sure, who sent them?"

"A secret admirer," Dee Dee said.

"No kidding?" Adam said. Once again he turned to Roy. "Ready?"

"Sure, I'll go get my bike," Roy said, getting up. "Anyone who wants to watch me make a video that's sure to get on 'America's Stupidest Home Videos' is welcome to come down to the park."

"I'll pass," Janine said. "I'm going Rollerblading with Muffy."

"I'd love to go, darling," Flora said to Roy. "But you know what it will do to my nerves. I simply can't bear watching one of my children risk breaking his neck."

Roy looked at Dee Dee. "How about you and Wordsworth?"

"Okay," Dee Dee said, "we'll be there in a little while."

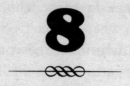

8

A little while later Dee Dee and I headed for the park.

"Didn't you think that was strange?" she asked in a low voice as we walked. She was being careful in case someone we couldn't see was watching us.

"Someone sending Janine the flowers?" I whispered.

"No, the way Adam acted. He didn't look interested or surprised by them. He wasn't even curious to know who sent them."

"I guess he just doesn't care," I said.

"I wonder," Dee Dee said.

It took a while to get through the park, as I had to stop and sniff lots of trees and bushes. Finally we got down to the rocky shoreline. Adam had set up his video camera on a tripod near the water's edge.

Wordsworth and the Tasty Treat Trick

"Where's Roy?" Dee Dee asked him.

"He should be coming any second now," Adam said, aiming the video camera.

"Coming from where?" Dee Dee asked.

"Over there." Adam pointed at the bike path that ran through the park. "Then he'll leave the path, cross the grass, go off that low wall, and across the rocks to that jump."

Adam pointed at a wooden ramp on the rocks near the water's edge. "The idea is to go off the ramp and sail over that last big rock. Then he'll land in the water."

Dee Dee looked at Adam like he was out of his mind. "Are you crazy? He'll *never* make it. If he doesn't crash going off the wall, then he's bound to lose his balance on the rocks or miss the ramp."

"That's the whole point," Adam said. "He's not supposed to succeed. The thing everyone loves so much about 'America's Stupidest Home Videos' is watching people fail."

"*Ya-hoo!*" someone shouted. We looked up and saw Roy racing along the bike path on his bike. He was wearing a helmet, a diving mask and snorkel, a life preserver, a bathing suit, his soccer shin guards, and diving flippers.

"Here we go." Adam got behind the video camera and followed the action.

"I can't believe he's really going to try this," Dee Dee groaned. "Mom was right. He's going to break his neck."

Roy rode off the path and across the grass. He went off the wall and hit the rocks. I was certain he was going to lose his balance then, but somehow he managed to stay up as he bounced over the rocks. The next thing we knew, he went up the wooden ramp and flew over the big rock.

Ker-splash! Roy landed in the sound and bobbed up and down in the water.

"He did it!" Dee Dee screeched, pumping her arms up and down triumphantly. "I can't believe he did it!"

"Of all the rotten luck," Adam muttered, shaking his head. "They'll never want this video now."

Roy swam to the rocks and climbed over them toward us, flippers flopping. He was dripping wet, and pulled the mask off his face.

"Too bad, Roy." Adam patted him on the shoulder.

Roy shrugged. "I guess we'll have to try something else."

"Well, I don't care whether it was good enough to get on 'America's Stupidest Home Videos' or not," Dee Dee said. "I thought it was great."

Roy gave her a broken smile. "Thanks, Dee Dee."

"But what about your bike?" she asked.

"It sank," Roy said. "I'm gonna go home and get some rope. I'll swim down and tie it to the bike and we'll pull it out. You guys can wait here."

Roy flopped off in his flippers, leaving wet tracks resembling those of a giant duck.

"Your brother's a real trouper," Adam said.

"Either that or he's a total bonehead," said Dee Dee.

Adam smiled and sat down on the rocks. The sailboats were out. "I never realized how beautiful it is here."

Dee Dee and I sat down next to him. Adam patted me on the head. "How's Wordsworth?"

"He's okay," Dee Dee said. She gave me a funny look and I knew what she was thinking about. "Hey, Adam, can I ask you something personal?"

"Sure."

"Do you remember when you kidnapped Wordsworth?" she asked.

"Well, sort of," Adam said. "I wasn't exactly playing with a full deck of cards, if you know what I mean."

"Then you don't remember?" Dee Dee asked.

"What? That I thought Wordsworth could talk?" Adam actually blushed. "I had a lot of crazy ideas back then. You don't have to remind me."

Dee Dee nodded slowly.

"So what's Janine going to do about the dance?" Adam asked.

"Not go, I guess."

"That's too bad," Adam said.

"No, it's not. She doesn't want to go."

"I didn't mean it was too bad for her," Adam said. "I meant it was too bad for someone else."

"Who?" Dee Dee asked. "Those guys who bet on her? I don't feel sorry for them."

"I didn't mean them, either," Adam said.

"Then who?"

Adam took a deep breath and let it out slowly. "If I tell you a secret, will you swear you won't tell a soul?"

"I swear," said Dee Dee.

"Not anyone in your family," Adam said. "And especially not Janine."

"Come on, Adam, enough with the big buildup," Dee Dee said impatiently. "The suspense is killing me."

"You really want to know who sent those flowers this morning?"

"Sure I—" Dee Dee's eyes widened and her mouth fell open. "*You?*"

Adam nodded.

Dee Dee frowned. "You want to win the bet?"

"No, no." Adam shook his head. "I have nothing

to do with the bet. The only reason I want to take her is because I . . . well, I . . . I'm crazy about her."

"Really?" Dee Dee gasped.

Adam stiffened. "You have to swear you won't tell anyone."

"But why are you telling me?" Dee Dee asked.

Adam took a deep breath and let it out in a long sigh. "Because I really, really want to take Janine to the dance. And I need your help to do it."

9

"My help?" Dee Dee's forehead wrinkled. "What can I do?"

"Shh!" Adam pressed his finger against his lips and nodded behind him. Roy had returned with a rope. He dove into the water and tied one end of it around the bike. Then he and Adam pulled the bike out of Bell Island Sound and we all headed back toward home.

"I still can't believe that stunt worked," Roy said. "I was certain I was going to crash before I hit the water."

"Too bad," Adam said.

"I guess I'll have to come up with something different," Dee Dee's brother said.

"Aren't you worried about getting hurt?" Dee Dee asked.

"A little," Roy said. "But it would be worth it to get on 'America's Stupidest Home Videos.'"

We got back to our house. Adam said he had to go to his house for a while. But before he left, he asked Dee Dee to think about what he'd said.

"What'd he say?" Roy asked after Adam left.

"Oh, uh, nothing important," Dee Dee said, remembering her promise.

Roy took the bike around to the back of the house to wash off the salt water with a hose. Meanwhile Dee Dee and I sat on the front steps and watched the cars go past on Soundview Avenue.

"What do you think, Wordsworth?" Dee Dee asked in a low voice.

"I think it's time for a snack," I said. "How about something radically different today? Like spareribs or a meatball fondue?"

"No, I meant about what Adam said."

"You mean, him being crazy about Janine?" I asked.

Dee Dee nodded. "Do you think we should help him?"

"But she said she doesn't want to go to the dance," I said.

"Maybe we could get her to change her mind," Dee Dee said. "What do you think?"

I scratched my ear with my rear paw and thought about it. "Yes, I think we should."

"Why?" Dee Dee asked.

"Because he brings me treats and scratches my tummy," I said. "That's the sign of a really good person. Not only that, but he helps Leyland in his workshop and cooks for your family. And of course, he's helping Roy come up with stunts for 'America's Stupidest Home Videos.' All in all, he's being very nice to us."

Dee Dee tucked her knees up under her chin and stared at the passing cars. "It's just so hard to believe that he's changed that much. I mean, what if all this is a trick?"

"What kind of trick?" I asked.

"Maybe he is in on the bet," Dee Dee said. "Maybe he's trying to trick us into helping him win the money."

"Does he hang around the yacht club?" I asked.

"No."

"Is he friendly with any of the guys who made the bet?" I asked.

Dee Dee shook her head. "No. I've never seen him hanging around with any of them."

"Then I doubt he's part of it."

"I wonder if there could be another reason why he'd do it," Dee Dee said.

"Why does there have to be another reason?" I asked. "Why do you have to be such a pessimist? Don't you believe that people can change?"

Dee Dee gave me a skeptical look.

"Take me, for example," I said. "I used to be a selfish, greedy, spoiled dog. All I cared about was having enough to eat and a comfortable place to sleep. Now look at me."

Dee Dee looked at me and smiled. "So, what's changed?"

I felt my jaw drop. "How can you say that? I'm a completely changed dog. I've lost weight. I'm more helpful. I go for walks without complaining."

"I was only joking." Dee Dee smiled and scratched my head affectionately. "It's just that I've always known that beneath that gruff exterior was a good dog. I'm not so sure that's true of Adam."

"If you never give him the chance, how will you know?" I asked.

Dee Dee sighed. "I guess this means we're going to help him get Janine to the dance."

"It's our duty," I said.

10

Clump! . . . Clomp! . . . Clump! A little while later Dee Dee and I were in the kitchen when we heard the sound of Janine clumping up the front steps in her Rollerblades. She got into the house, skated down the hall, and joined us. Her face was red, and little beads of perspiration dotted her forehead. She rolled up to the refrigerator and took out a big plastic bottle of Orangina.

"Wow, what a day." She was still huffing and puffing as she poured herself a glass of Orangina and skated over to the kitchen table. "You really ought to get outside, Dee Dee."

"I will," Dee Dee said, "but there's something I want to talk to you about first."

"Let me guess." Janine took a big gulp. "There's something of mine you want to wear?"

"No," Dee Dee said. "I just want to know if you really think it's a good idea to be so mean to boys?"

Janine frowned. "What are you talking about?"

"Aren't you worried you'll get a reputation?"

"Worried? I *hope* I get a reputation," Janine said. "A reputation for not being interested in boys. Then maybe they'll leave me alone."

"But at your age aren't girls supposed to be interested in boys?"

"I really don't care what girls are *supposed* to do," Janine said with a shrug.

"What if you change?" Dee Dee asked. "Just because you don't like boys now doesn't mean you won't like them someday. Maybe someday you'll want a boy to ask you out, but nobody will because they'll all think you hate guys. People change, you know. Look at Adam."

Janine gave her little sister a funny look. "Are you feeling okay?"

"Don't you think Adam's changed?" Dee Dee asked.

"It looks like he has."

"Well, you may change, too," Dee Dee said. "Someday you may want a boyfriend more than anything in the world, and you won't be able to find a single one."

Janine finished her glass of Orangina and got up. "Know what I think?"

"What?"

"I think it's time you got a life and stopped worrying about mine." Janine rolled away back down the hall.

Dee Dee gazed down at me with a defeated look on her face. "Guess that didn't work."

"Don't give up so easily," I whispered.

"But what can I say to her?"

"If she won't go to the dance for her own sake, maybe she'll go for Adam's."

"Get real, Wordsworth." Dee Dee gave me a dubious look.

"Hey, it's worth a try," I said.

Janine had gone upstairs to take a shower. Dee Dee and I climbed the stairs. Now that I was a slim, svelte dog, I could get up and down the steps pretty easily.

We got up to Janine's room. As usual, the floor was littered with her clothes, CDs, magazines, and other things. The bathroom door was closed. We heard the hissing shower sound stop. A moment later Janine came back into the bedroom wrapped in a towel. When she saw Dee Dee she stopped.

"What are you doing in here?"

"I, uh, wanted to talk to you about something," Dee Dee said.

"Boys again?" Janine guessed.

"Well, one in particular," Dee Dee said. "Adam."

"What about him?"

"How do you think he must feel?"

"About what?" Janine asked.

"About his self-image," Dee Dee said. "I mean, he's not a creep anymore, so he can't hang out with his old creep friends. But he doesn't have any new friends either. The only person he ever hangs around with is Roy. I bet he's really lonely."

"Please make your point," Janine said impatiently.

"I think it would be really nice if we did something for his self-image," Dee Dee said. "Something that would show other people that he's a really nice guy now."

"Uh, Dee Dee, let me remind you that it wasn't that long ago that he climbed up a tree and looked in my bedroom window," Janine said. "I don't exactly have warm feelings toward him."

"But he's changed," Dee Dee said. "Admit it."

"Okay, so maybe he has. What about it?"

"Well . . ." Dee Dee took a deep breath and glanced nervously at me. "You could go to the dance with him."

"Go to the dance . . . with Adam Pickney?" Janine's eyes went wide. Her mouth opened. Dee Dee winced. I covered my ears with my paws. This wasn't going to be pretty.

11

"What a great idea!" Janine gasped.

"Huh?" Dee Dee looked shocked. I took my paws off my ears. Had I heard her right? Janine actually *liked* the idea of going to the dance with Adam?

"It's brilliant!" Janine cried happily. "It's fabulous! It's—" Her eyes suddenly narrowed. "Wait a minute. Are you sure Adam isn't in on the bet?"

"I'm positive," Dee Dee said.

"Then it's perfect!" Janine smiled and hugged her sister. "Dee Dee, you're a genius!"

"I am?" Dee Dee was clearly confused.

"Yes. Now I won't have to worry about all those guys bothering me," Janine said. "As soon as they hear I'm going to the dance with Adam, they'll leave me alone."

On the kitchen counter, the phone machine

clicked on. Even though Leyland had turned off the ringer, we still knew when someone was calling because of the clicking sound the phone machine made.

"I'm going to get that!" Janine grabbed the phone. "Hello? . . . Oh, hi, Chuck. . . . Well, I'm afraid I have bad news for you. I've decided to go to the dance with Adam. . . . Adam Pickney, my next-door neighbor . . . A dirtbag? Oh, no, he's really changed. He's great. . . . Sure, go ahead and tell all the other guys. . . . No, I'm sure I won't change my mind. I promised Adam I'd go with him and I'd never break my promise. . . . Okay, bye."

Janine hung up, looking happier than she'd looked in months. "Oh, Dee Dee, this is the best thing that's ever happened to me! How can I thank you?"

Dee Dee was still in shock. "Are you *really* going to go to the dance with Adam?"

"Absolutely," Janine said. "I mean, it won't be such a big deal. Only . . ." She hesitated.

"What?" Dee Dee asked.

"I sure wish he'd wear better clothes," Janine said.

12

"Janine says she'll go to the dance with you," Dee Dee said that night. "But she really wishes you'd wear better clothes."

It was dinnertime and Adam had come over to make us hamburgers. He was wearing a green polo shirt, tan bermuda shorts, and green over-the-calf socks. Still, I thought Dee Dee could have been a little more discreet.

"What's wrong with these clothes?" Adam asked.

"Nothing," Dee Dee said. "It's just that you look like someone's grandfather who's just come back from the golf course."

"I do?"

"Uh-huh."

"Well, it's really important not to give in to peer pressure," Adam said. "That was a problem I used to

51

have. I can't let myself get sucked into it again. I have to maintain my individuality."

"Can I be direct, Adam?" Dee Dee asked.

"Sure."

"Maintaining your individuality is one thing," Dee Dee said. "Looking like a total dork is another. You don't want to embarrass Janine, do you?"

"Well, no, of course not. I'd never want to do that," Adam said.

"Then take my advice and get some new clothes for the dance."

"But . . . I don't know what to get," he said. "I mean, I definitely don't want to look like a dork. But I don't want to look like everyone else either."

Dee Dee rubbed her chin and thought. "You know what I'm going to do? I'm going to take you shopping."

13

The next day was the day before the dance. Dee Dee and Adam went shopping. I wasn't allowed to go with them. Dee Dee would have taken me, but she said that I wouldn't be allowed in stores. I didn't really care. I don't like shopping, except in supermarkets.

They were gone for a long time. Finally they came home carrying a bunch of shopping bags.

"Have you been a good boy while we were away?" Dee Dee asked, rubbing my head.

Groof! I barked like a dumb happy dog and wagged my tail.

"Hey." Adam reached into his pocket and tossed me a tasty treat. "Almost forgot!"

"Okay," Dee Dee said. "Adam and I are going over to his house. Adam's going to try on his new things and we'll see what looks the best. I'll be back in a little while."

That was fine with me. I lay down on the kitchen floor again.

"I think Wordsworth should come with us," Adam said.

"Why?" asked Dee Dee.

"He hasn't seen you all day. Wouldn't it be mean of you to leave him again so soon?"

"Oh, Wordsworth doesn't mind," Dee Dee said. "As long as he knows I'll be back to give him dinner."

"But I insist," Adam said. "I really want him to come to my house."

Dee Dee gave him a funny look. "Well, if you really feel strongly about it." She turned to me. "Come on, Wordsworth, let's go."

I got up and followed them. I had never been allowed inside the Pickneys' house before, but I assumed they'd have a nice soft rug to take a nap on. We left our house and started up the flagstone walk to the Pickneys' front door.

"Are you sure about this?" Dee Dee asked. "I sort of remember you once saying your parents hated animals."

"They'll never know," Adam said. "They're away for the week." He opened the front door and held it for us. Dee Dee and I went in.

Wordsworth and the Tasty Treat Trick

"Wow!" Dee Dee looked around with wide eyes. Unlike the Chandlers', the inside of the Pickneys' house was richly decorated, and perfectly neat and spotless. Every couch and chair looked brand-new, as if no one had ever sat in it. The pictures on the walls hung straight. Books and magazines were in neat rows and piles. Adam led us into the living room.

"Tell you what," he said. "You guys wait here. I'll go in another room and start trying things on. Then I'll come out and you can tell me what you think."

"Okay." Dee Dee sat down in an old chair.

"Uh, don't sit there," Adam said. "That's, er, my father's special chair. You'd better sit on the couch."

Dee Dee sat down in a corner of the couch.

"Okay, I'll be right back," Adam said, and left the room.

I lay down on a sunny spot on the living-room rug and closed my eyes. Just as I'd hoped, the Pickneys' rugs were much thicker and softer than the rugs at our house. I took a short nap. When I opened my eyes again, Dee Dee was still sitting on the couch. I gave her a curious look. *Where was Adam?*

"I don't know, Wordsworth," she whispered, as if she could read my mind. "I guess it takes him a long time to change clothes."

I didn't know if she wanted me to answer her. We were in a strange house. There was always a chance

Adam might hear. The sunny spot had moved across the floor, so I got up and moved to it.

A moment later Adam came in wearing a blue-and-white-checked shirt, brown slacks, and black shoes. "Well, what do you think?"

Dee Dee grimaced slightly. "I think they're all nice, just not together."

"Oh." Adam's shoulders sagged. "Guess I better try something else. By the way, could you sit more in the middle of the couch?"

Dee Dee frowned. "Why?"

"Uh, I just want to be able to see you better when I come out in my new clothes," Adam said. "So I can see your first impression."

"Okay." Dee Dee slid over to the middle of the couch.

"And do you think Wordsworth could move over and sit at your feet?" Adam asked.

Dee Dee scowled.

"I want to see his reaction, too," Adam explained.

"You want to see Wordsworth's reaction?"

"Yes, I consider him my friend, too," Adam said. "He has a very expressive face."

I was rather flattered. I liked the idea of being a fashion critic. Maybe someday I would go to Paris and be part of the haute couture world. I would wear sunglasses and a raincoat and nothing underneath. I would say "fabulous, darling" a lot.

56

Wordsworth and the Tasty Treat Trick

"Okay," Dee Dee said. Then she called to me. "Wordsworth, could you come over here?"

I got up and sat at Dee Dee's feet.

"Great," Adam said. "I'll be right back."

14

"Is it my imagination, or is he being weird?" Dee Dee whispered after Adam left the room.

"It's not your imagination," I whispered back.

"What do you think is going on?"

"I don't have a clue."

This time it took even longer for Adam to return.

Dee Dee fidgeted on the couch. "What in the world is he doing?"

"You got me," I said with a yawn.

Dee Dee got up. Near the couch was a tall bookcase. She went over to it and began to look at the books.

Suddenly Adam came in. This time he was wearing a green cotton sweater, red slacks, and yellow boat shoes.

"Tah-dah!" he said, spreading his arms. "What do you think?"

Dee Dee rolled her eyes. "I think you better try again."

Adam's shoulders sagged. "This isn't so great, huh?"

"Adam, when you were a dirtbag, how did you know what to wear?" Dee Dee asked.

"Easy," he said. "I always wore black. By the way, would you mind sitting on the couch?"

"Why?" Dee Dee asked.

"Well, it's my mom," Adam said. "She'll know if you touch the bookshelf. She's really sensitive to fingerprints."

"Oh." Dee Dee went back to the couch and sat down.

"In the center, okay?"

Dee Dee slid over to the center of the couch.

"Great, I'll be right back." Adam left again.

Dee Dee let out a big sigh. "This is really weird, Wordsworth. I've never heard of someone being sensitive to fingerprints before."

"Maybe she's a very 'touchy' person," I quipped.

Dee Dee grinned. "Very funny, Wordsworth. I guess we're in for another long wait."

"Might as well make the most of it," I said, rolling onto my back. "How about a nice tummy scratch?"

"Sure." Dee Dee bent over and scratched my

tummy. "Isn't it funny how things change? Adam used to be our biggest enemy. Now he's our best friend. Everyone in the family likes him."

"It reaffirms your faith in humanity," I said. "It reaffirms my faith in food."

"Isn't it neat that he's going to the dance with Janine?" Dee Dee asked. "Once other people see him with her, they'll know he's changed. I bet he's going to be really popular."

"If he ever figures out what clothes to wear," I said.

"I know. Isn't it weird how some people have no sense of style?"

"We canines never have that problem," I said. "We always look great in our coats."

"Hardy-har-har." Dee Dee smirked. "You may have lost weight, Wordsworth, but you sure haven't lost your ability to tell a bad joke."

"I've got another one for you," I said. "What kind of dog can tell time?"

"Hmmm." Dee Dee rubbed her chin and thought. "I know! A watchdog!"

"How'd you guess?" I asked.

"We humans aren't so dumb either," Dee Dee said. "Now here's one for you. Why do dogs make such bad dancers?"

"Uh . . . Because we never take dancing lessons?" I guessed.

Wordsworth and the Tasty Treat Trick

"No, because you have two left feet," Dee Dee said.

"Two left feet?" I didn't get it. "But we have two right feet, too."

Dee Dee rolled her eyes. "Forget it, Wordsworth, it was just a joke."

Adam came back into the living room. This time he was wearing a pair of dark green slacks, a white shirt with a blue cotton sweater over his shoulders, and deck shoes.

Dee Dee sat up straight. "Oh, Adam, that looks great!"

Woof! Woof! I barked in agreement.

"Then it's settled," Adam said. "Thanks, guys." He went over to the front door and held it open. "See you soon."

Dee Dee looked surprised. It seemed like Adam suddenly wanted us to leave.

"Aren't you coming over to cook dinner tonight?" she asked.

"Gee, I don't think I'll be able to make it," Adam said. "But I'll see you tomorrow, okay?"

"Okay. Come on, Wordsworth." Dee Dee and I went out the door and Adam slammed it behind us.

"That's funny," Dee Dee said once we got outside. "I wonder why he wanted us to leave so fast?"

15

The next morning I slept late as usual. Then Dee Dee came down to the kitchen and gave me breakfast.

"How'd you sleep?" she asked with a yawn.

"Like a log," I said, stretching.

"Change the L to a D and you slept like a dog," she said.

"I'll remember that."

"Know what today is?" she asked.

"National Feed Your Dog Pizza Day?"

"No, it's the day of the dance, silly."

Flora came in and made herself a mug of tea. Janine came in wearing a baggy T-shirt. She took a package of strawberry Pop-Tarts out of the pantry and sat down at the kitchen table. For a moment the three women of the Chandler family were quiet.

"Know what's weird?" Janine asked with a yawn.

Wordsworth and the Tasty Treat Trick

"Dad turned the phone back on last night, but the phone hasn't rung once."

"Do you think there's something wrong with the telephone line?" Flora asked.

"No, I think everyone's heard that I'm going to the dance with Adam and they've given up trying to win the bet," Janine said. She smiled at her little sister. "Dee Dee, that was a stroke of genius."

"I have more good news," Dee Dee said. "You know how Adam has been wearing those nerdy clothes? Well, yesterday we went shopping and I got him to buy some nice things for tonight."

Just then Roy came into the kitchen. "Hey, guys, anyone seen Adam?"

"No, dear, he hasn't come over yet this morning," Flora said.

"I better call him," Roy said, picking up the phone. "We're supposed to get together today and work on another video for 'America's Stupidest Home Videos.' The ASHV van is going to be here any day."

"Got any new ideas?" Dee Dee asked while her brother dialed.

"Yeah, I'm thinking about making some wings out of plywood and then riding my bike off the roof," Roy said.

"With your luck, you'll actually fly," said Janine.

Roy frowned and hung up the phone. "That's funny, he's not answering."

"Maybe he went out," Janine said.

Now Leyland came into the kitchen. "Good morning, family. Has anyone seen my apprentice?"

"He's not home," Roy said.

"That's odd." Leyland looked puzzled. "He was supposed to come over this morning and help put the finishing touches on the new improved Chandler E-Z Glide Self-Propelled Riding Vacuum."

"You guys are unreal," Janine suddenly said.

The wrinkles on Leyland's forehead deepened. "Why, dear?"

"You all act like Adam belongs to us," Janine said. "He *does* have a life of his own, you know."

"You're right, Janine," Dee Dee said. "Anyway, I'm going to take Wordsworth for a walk in the park. Come on, Wordsworth."

I got up and went over to the sliding door while Dee Dee got my leash. Walks in the park were still not one of my favorite activities, but I'd come to accept them as a necessary evil in the struggle against obesity.

"You know what's funny?" Dee Dee said when we got to the park.

"A cat trying to bark?" I guessed.

"No, I meant about Adam," she said. "Janine was right. We don't own Adam. He has a right to do whatever he pleases. But when he's not around I sort of miss him. How about you?"

"I miss those tasty treats he brings," I said.

Dee Dee put her hands on her hips and shook her head. "I should have known."

We walked a little more.

"Oh, look!" Dee Dee suddenly gasped. She went over onto the grass and picked up something round and rather dirty. "An old tennis ball."

She bent down and held it to my nose. It smelled like bad dog breath.

"Okay, Wordsworth, fetch!" Dee Dee threw the ball across the grass.

I stood and watched it roll away.

"Go on, fetch!" Dee Dee said excitedly.

"Get real," I muttered.

"Oh, come on, Wordsworth." Dee Dee looked disappointed. "I thought you'd changed."

"Let me ask you a question," I said. "And tell me the truth. Would *you* put that ball in *your* mouth?"

Dee Dee made a face. "Yuck."

"I rest my case," I said.

We were on our way home from the park when we saw Adam going up the walk to his house, carrying something in his hand.

Wordsworth and the Tasty Treat Trick

"Hey, Adam!" Dee Dee called.

Adam wheeled around and looked surprised. He quickly hid the object behind his back. "Oh, uh, hi, Dee Dee."

"Everyone was looking for you this morning," Dee Dee said. "My dad and Roy thought you were going to work with them."

"Oh, well, I had to go out," he said.

Adam was clearly acting nervous about something. I noticed that he was also wearing his old black clothes again, along with his earrings and nose ring. Curious about what he was hiding behind his back, I walked behind him.

But he kept turning so that I couldn't see what he was hiding.

Groof! Groof! I knew what he was hiding—more tasty treats!

"Forget it, Wordsworth," Adam said.

"Are you excited about the dance?" Dee Dee asked.

"Oh, gee, that reminds me," Adam said. "Something came up. I can't go after all."

16

Dee Dee looked shocked. "But you have to! It's tonight! You can't back out now!"

"Sorry," Adam said. "Like I said, something came up."

"But Janine's counting on you. I worked so hard to get her to say yes. You bought those clothes. Everyone expects you to go."

I kept trying to circle around behind Adam to see what he was hiding, but he kept turning to prevent me from seeing.

"Too bad," Adam said.

"But Adam, really, you *have* to go." Dee Dee sounded really disappointed.

"Hey, things change, okay?" Adam snapped. "Now get out of my face."

With a surprised look on her face, Dee Dee

stepped back and studied him. "Why are you wearing those old yucky black clothes? I thought you said you'd changed."

"Hey, just get off my case, okay?" Adam growled.

"What about Roy and my father?" Dee Dee asked. "Roy's waiting for you to help him make a video, and my father expects you to help him with his invention."

"Well, that's just too bad," Adam said.

Just then we heard the rattling, scraping sound of Rollerblades. Looking up the street, I saw two guys skating toward us. One of them looked familiar. It was Chuck, the guy who'd tried so hard to get Janine to go to the dance with him.

"Hey, it's Adam Pickney, the man of the year," Chuck said, stopping on the street near us.

"Hey, Chuck, hey, Max," Adam said.

"How'd you do it, dude?" asked Max, a boy with red hair in a mushroom cut.

"Do what?" Adam asked.

"Get Janine Chandler to go to the dance with you."

"Yeah, dude," said Chuck. "You beat out fifteen guys who were all killing themselves to get her to go."

"Well, I just asked," Adam said with a shrug and a smile.

"Come off it, Pickney," Max said. "We all just asked. You *had* to do something more than that."

"Tell them about the flowers," Dee Dee said.

Adam grinned. It was obvious that he enjoyed being the center of attention.

"He sent her the most beautiful bouquet of flowers," Dee Dee said.

Chuck and Max looked at each other.

"Darn," Max said. "Why didn't I think of that?"

"Adam, I have to hand it to you," Chuck said. "You are one cool dude. I mean, from now on Adam Pickney is a legend around here."

"Yeah, the guy who finally got Janine Chandler to go on a date," said Max.

By now Adam was glowing with pride. But he'd also forgotten about me. I was able to sneak around behind him and see what he was hiding behind his back. It wasn't a tasty treat, it was a videocassette. *Darn!*

"So, dude, I guess we'll see you and Janine at the dance tonight," Chuck said.

"Depend on it," Adam replied.

"Later." Chuck and Max started to skate away.

Dee Dee turned to Adam. "I thought you weren't going to go to the dance," she said.

"And miss the chance to become a living legend?" Adam smiled. "I guess I just changed my mind."

17

Adam went into his house and Dee Dee started to lead me back toward ours. "That was weird, Wordsworth," she said. "Adam wasn't acting very nice at all. He was acting just like the 'old' Adam."

"I know," I said. "And did you notice he didn't give me a treat?"

"What was he hiding from us?"

"It looked like a videotape to me," I said.

"Why do you think he was hiding it?" Dee Dee asked.

"I can't imagine."

"Well, maybe we're just being too sensitive," Dee Dee said. "Everybody's entitled to a bad mood now and then. And he did agree to go to the dance after all."

Maybe she was right. Even good people had bad

moods once in a while. We got home and found Roy and his father arguing.

"Plywood wings?" Leyland gasped. "That's ridiculous. They'll never fly."

"But that's the whole point, Dad," Roy tried to explain. "It's not supposed to fly. It's supposed to crash."

"This is preposterous," Leyland replied. "The only way you'll have a prayer of flying off the roof is with Mylar wings. You're in luck, son, I've got a large roll of Mylar in the shop. If you're going to fly off our roof, it's going to be with a set of *real* wings."

Leyland marched down to the basement. Roy gave us a hopeless look.

"You know how Dad gets," Dee Dee said sympathetically. "You better go downstairs."

"I guess no matter what he makes, I can always get them to crash," Roy said.

After that we forgot about Adam for the rest of the day. Dee Dee played with some friends and I decided to take a long nap in Dee Dee's room.

I woke around dinnertime to the sound of Dee Dee and Janine arguing in Janine's room.

"Oh, please let me watch?" Dee Dee was begging her older sister.

"No," Janine replied.

I stretched and yawned and wandered into

Janine's room. Dee Dee's big sister was sitting at her desk. Propped up in front of her was a small round mirror with small white lightbulbs around its edge. Dee Dee was standing behind her.

"But if you don't let me watch, I'll never learn," Dee Dee said.

"You're too young to learn."

"Then at least let me watch," Dee Dee begged. "I never get to see this. Mom and you never wear makeup."

Grooof! I barked in agreement.

Janine gave me an exasperated look. "What's *he* want?"

"He wants to watch, too," Dee Dee said.

Janine sighed and shook her head. "I sincerely believe that this is the strangest family on earth. Okay, you can both watch."

For the next half hour we watched her brush her hair in various styles and apply makeup to her eyes and face. Then she put on a slinky red dress.

"Oh, Janine, you look like a movie star!" Dee Dee cried.

"Give me a break." Her big sister rolled her eyes.

Dee Dee turned to me. "What do you think, Wordsworth?"

The truth is, I rarely care about the way humans look. No matter how much they paint and costume themselves, they never look nearly as pretty as an attractive canine female. However, Janine did look stunning.

Groof! Groof! I voiced my approval.

Ding! Dong! The front doorbell rang.

"That must be Adam!" Dee Dee gasped excitedly.

"Do me a favor and go tell him I'm not ready," Janine said.

"But you are ready," said Dee Dee.

"Of course I am," Janine said. "But that's not the point. You never want to look too eager. You *always* make men wait."

Dee Dee and I went downstairs. She pulled open the front door. Adam was standing there, wearing the clothes he and Dee Dee had bought the day before. But he was also wearing some earrings.

"She ready?" he asked.

"She said she'd be down in a moment," Dee Dee said. "Are you in a better mood now?"

"Huh? What are you talking about?" Adam scowled at her.

"You weren't in a very good mood this morning."

"Oh, yeah." Adam grinned. "I'm in a *great* mood now, thanks to you and Wordsworth."

Groof! Groof! I hoped that meant he'd brought some tasty treats with him. But Adam just ignored me.

Wordsworth and the Tasty Treat Trick

Roy came to the door. "Hey, Adam, you should see the pair of wings Dad and I made today! Think you'll be able to tape me flying off the roof tomorrow? The ASHV van's supposed to be here the day after."

"Uh, we'll have to see tomorrow," Adam said, looking at his watch. "So where's Janine?"

"I told you she's coming," Dee Dee said. "What's the rush?"

"Uh, nothing," Adam said.

"Ah, there you are," Leyland said, coming to the door. "I thought you were going to work with me on the new version of the Chandler E-Z Glide Self-Propelled Vacuum today."

"Something came up," Adam said.

"What about tomorrow?" Dee Dee's dad asked.

"I'm afraid not," Adam said.

"Then perhaps the day after that?" Leyland asked.

Adam shook his head. "To tell you the truth, Mr. Chandler, I think you're gonna have to find a new apprentice. I've got a really big deal coming up."

"Oh, well, I'm sorry to hear that." Leyland looked disappointed. Then he brightened. "I hope it's something good."

"Oh, it is, believe me," Adam said with a smirk. "It's great."

That bothered me. Why was he smirking?

Adam glanced at his watch again and looked annoyed. "What's taking her so long?"

Now Flora joined everyone at the door. "Janine!" she called upstairs. "It's not polite to keep your date waiting."

"Coming!" Janine called back. A moment later she came to the top of the stairs. By the front door, everyone let out a collective gasp.

"Darling, you look wonderful!" said Leyland.

"Hot tuna!" cried Roy.

"You're so grown up!" sniffed Flora.

"Sexy!" yelled Dee Dee with a big grin as Janine started down the stairs.

Only one person hadn't spoken. I looked up at Adam. His eyes were wide and his jaw was slack. He looked like he'd just been struck by lightning.

18

⸙

Janine came down the stairs. Flora kissed her on the cheek.

"Have a wonderful time, darling."

"No drinking and driving," Leyland reminded her.

"And no kissing!" added Dee Dee.

"Dee Dee!" Janine gasped and turned a little red. Then she stopped in front of Adam. "Ready?"

Adam still appeared to be in some kind of fog. He couldn't seem to take his eyes off her. "Uh . . . Uh . . . yeah."

Janine slid her arm through his and they went down the front steps together.

"She's so grown up!" Flora whispered, and wiped a tear from her eye.

Leyland put his arm around her shoulder. "Now, now, darling, we always knew this would happen."

"Did you see Adam?" Roy asked. "He looked totally gaga when he saw her."

"Gaga?" Leyland frowned. "Can that be translated?"

"Sure," Roy said. "He flipped. He's a goner."

"I think Roy's trying to say that Adam discovered a newfound affection for our daughter," Flora explained.

"Like love at first sight," Roy said.

"But he's seen her before," said Leyland.

"Not looking like that," said Roy.

"Oh, well, whatever will be, will be," Leyland said, closing the front door. "I suppose we might as well spend a quiet evening and wait until tomorrow morning to get a full report."

That sounded good to me. I headed back to the kitchen, looking forward to getting some sleep. I lay down on my doggy bed and closed my eyes. I was just starting to drift away when a voice whispered, "Wordsworth, wake up."

I opened my eyes. Dee Dee was kneeling next to me.

"Come on, we're going," she whispered.

"Where?" I asked with a yawn.

"The dance, where else?"

"Why?"

Dee Dee pressed her lips together. "Because I have a funny feeling something isn't right."

19

Dee Dee told her parents she was taking me for a walk.

"Why do you think something isn't right?" I asked as we started toward the club. The sun was setting and above us the clouds were tinted pink and light purple.

"Because I do," Dee Dee said. "Adam was acting very strangely."

"Roy said it was love at first sight."

"I'm not so sure," Dee Dee said. "Before Janine came downstairs, he seemed very impatient."

"Maybe he couldn't wait to see her."

"It didn't seem that way to me," Dee Dee said. "It was more like he couldn't wait to get the dance over with, like he had something more important in mind."

Wordsworth and the Tasty Treat Trick

"But it doesn't matter," I said. "Once Janine came downstairs, nothing else mattered to him."

"I'm not sure, Wordsworth. I'm just not sure."

Ahead of us was the yacht club. It looks like a big old mansion with a red roof. In the back, a broad green lawn slopes down to the water, where all the sailboats are moored. I slowed down. "This doesn't make sense. I'm not allowed in the club."

"Don't worry," Dee Dee said. "I'll get you in."

Dee Dee led me to the big wooden front doors of the clubhouse. Again I hesitated.

"We're going in the front?" I whispered.

"Just for a second," Dee Dee whispered back.

Inside the front doors Dee Dee made a sharp left and went through another door leading to a set of stairs. "Come on," she whispered, starting up the stairs.

"Where're we going?" I whispered, following her up the steps. Everything smelled very old and dusty. I got the feeling these stairs weren't used very often.

"Upstairs," Dee Dee said. "We used to play up there on rainy days when we were younger. There are some old offices on the second floor that no one uses anymore. We can watch the dance from there."

We got up to the second floor and Dee Dee led me down a dark hall and into a room with a desk and a large chair with a high back. On the far side of the room was a floor-to-ceiling window that looked out over the ballroom. Dee Dee and I pressed our noses against the glass and looked down.

"You sure we won't be seen?" I whispered.

"Not as long as we keep the lights off," Dee Dee whispered back. "Look, there's Janine!"

Down on the ballroom floor, Janine was standing with some other girls, talking. Adam stood nearby, his eyes glued to Dee Dee's sister.

"Do you believe it, Wordsworth?" Dee Dee giggled. "Adam can't take his eyes off her."

It was true. Adam followed Janine around like— you'll excuse the expression—a trained dog. He got her punch and cookies, he helped her into her seat when she sat, he never took his eyes off her when they danced.

"Who would have thought Adam could be such a perfect gentleman?" Dee Dee whispered.

"But I thought you thought something was wrong," I whispered back.

"I did," Dee Dee said. "Now I'm not so sure."

"Then we can go?" I asked. It made me nervous to be in the yacht club. Dogs were definitely not allowed. I was afraid that if I got caught they'd make me walk the plank.

"I want to stay and watch," Dee Dee said. "Maybe someday I'll—"

Wordsworth and the Tasty Treat Trick

Before she could finish the sentence, the door behind us swung open. Dee Dee and I spun around. A man in a dark green uniform stepped into the room and shone a flashlight on us.

"What are you doing in here?" he asked.

20

"Uh, nothing," Dee Dee stammered. "We were just watching the dance."

The man aimed the flashlight at me and I squinted in the bright light.

"I heard voices," he said. "There's another person in here somewhere."

The flashlight swept around the room. Dee Dee glanced nervously at me.

"Where is he?" the man asked.

"Who?" Dee Dee asked back.

"Don't get wise with me, young lady," the guard snapped angrily. "I heard you talking to someone else."

"Just to my dog," Dee Dee replied innocently.

"Well, you're not supposed to be in here," the guard said. "And neither is your dog."

"Okay, we'll go," Dee Dee said.

"You sure will," the guard said. "And don't let me ever catch you up here again."

The next morning everyone except Janine came down to the kitchen earlier than usual.

"Were you up last night when she came in?" Dee Dee asked her parents eagerly.

"I heard her come in," Leyland said, "but I was in bed. I didn't speak to her."

"I wonder how it went," Flora said.

"I'm sure it went great," Dee Dee said, giving me a wink.

A little while later Janine trudged into the kitchen wearing a white tennis shirt and shorts. Her eyes looked puffy from lack of sleep.

"Wow," Dee Dee said with a grin. "Looks like someone was out late last night."

Janine yawned. "Is there any coffee?"

"Of course not," Flora said. "None of us drink it."

"We do now." Janine yawned again. "I've got tennis in twenty minutes and I have to wake up fast."

She went to the pantry and found an old jar of instant coffee. She poured some in a mug, then added some hot water and sugar. Meanwhile the rest of the family sat quietly at the kitchen table and watched her.

"What's everyone looking at?" Janine asked.

"We're waiting to hear," Roy said.

"Hear what?" Janine asked.

"How your date with Adam went," Dee Dee said.

Janine rolled her eyes and took a sip of coffee. "It was okay. No big deal."

The kitchen grew quiet.

"That's it?" Leyland asked. "Just no big deal?"

"Uh-huh." Janine nodded.

"Do you think you'll see him again?" Roy asked.

"I don't know how I could avoid it," Janine said. "He's over here almost every day."

Briiiinnnggg! The phone rang.

Janine smiled. "Well, at least it won't be some guy begging me to go to the dance."

Roy jumped up and answered the phone. "Hello? Oh, hi, Adam. Yeah, she's right here." Roy put his hand over the receiver. Everyone thought he was going to hand it to Janine, but instead he held it toward Dee Dee. "He wants to talk to you."

"Me?" Dee Dee looked surprised.

"That's what he said." Roy handed her the phone.

"Hello?" Dee Dee pressed the receiver to her ear. "Uh, what? . . . Why? . . . Well, okay . . . Sure. Bye."

She hung up, frowning.

Wordsworth and the Tasty Treat Trick

"What'd he want?" Roy asked.

"He wants Wordsworth and me to come right over," Dee Dee said. She looked very puzzled. "He said it was very important."

21

A few minutes later we went up the walk to Adam's house and knocked on his front door. Adam opened it. He was wearing jeans and a T-shirt. His eyes looked puffy and tired, too.

"Hi, Adam, what's up?" Dee Dee asked.

"I want to show you something," he said. "Come in."

He led us to the den and turned on a TV. Then he flicked on a VCR underneath it.

"What's going on?" Dee Dee asked.

"Just give me a second," Adam said.

A slightly fuzzy, black-and-white picture flickered onto the TV screen. It had obviously been taken by an amateur with a video camera. Suddenly it came into focus and I could see Dee Dee and me sitting on the couch in Adam's living room. It must have been the day we'd come over to watch him try on clothes.

On the video, Dee Dee let out a big sigh. "This is really weird, Wordsworth. I've never heard of someone being sensitive to fingerprints before."

"I guess she's just a very 'touchy' person," I quipped.

Dee Dee grinned. "Very funny, Wordsworth. I guess we're in for another long wait."

"Might as well make the most of it," I said, rolling onto my back. "How about a nice tummy scratch?"

Now, in the Pickneys' den, Dee Dee and I stared at each other in shock. Adam had us talking on tape!

22

Adam turned off the television and VCR. Then he turned to Dee Dee and me.

"I . . . I don't understand," Dee Dee stammered.

"It's pretty obvious," Adam replied. "This time I've really got you two. I mean, there'll be no doubt now."

Neither Dee Dee nor I moved or said a word. We were still in shock. Finally Dee Dee said, "Why?"

"Why?" Adam laughed. "Get real, kid. Your dog is worth a fortune. I mean, millions and millions of dollars. 'America's Stupidest Home Videos' is gonna be here any day now and I'm gonna cash in big time. They'll kill for this tape."

"But I thought you changed," Dee Dee gasped.

"Sure, I did," Adam said. "I got smart. The whole time I was away, all I could think about was how rich I was gonna get. But I had to come up with a plan."

"But what about those nerdy clothes and cooking meals for us?" Dee Dee asked. "What about helping Roy make his video and helping my father with his inventions?"

"It was all part of the plan," Adam said. "I knew I had to get in good with your family and make you all believe that I'd changed. I had to get you to trust me. Once I did that, the rest was easy. All I had to do was wear those nerdy clothes and convince you that I needed your help to get new ones."

"But what about the bet?" Dee Dee asked.

"I had nothing to do with it," Adam said. "But it fit into my plans perfectly."

Dee Dee nodded sadly. "So you tricked us. And now you're going to sell the tape and get rich. And the whole world will find out about Wordsworth. Scientists will take him away from us and study his brain."

I snuggled up to Dee Dee and tried not to whimper with fear as I glared angrily at Adam. *Traitor! Cad! Double-crosser!*

"Maybe," Adam said.

"Maybe?" Dee Dee repeated, puzzled.

Adam took a deep breath and let it out in a long slow sigh. "Did Janine say anything about last night?"

"No. Why?"

Wrinkles appeared on Adam's forehead. "Nothing at all?"

"She just said it was okay, no big deal."

Adam pursed his lips. "Darn. I had a feeling she'd feel that way. The thing is, I was really nervous and stiff. She didn't get a chance to see the real me."

"So what?" Dee Dee said. "You didn't even want to go to the dance with her. You wouldn't have gone if Chuck and Max didn't say that you'd become a living legend."

"I know." Adam sat down and clasped his hands. He suddenly looked very earnest. "But then something happened."

"What?" Dee Dee asked.

Adam looked up at her. "I know you won't believe me, but I . . . I fell in love."

"*What?*" Dee Dee gasped in total shock.

Adam's face hardened as if he thought maybe she was making fun of him. "You heard me."

Dee Dee studied him. "Is this another trick?"

Adam looked surprised at the suggestion.

"I don't think so," I said.

Dee Dee made a face at me, but I didn't see why I shouldn't talk. After all, Adam already had me talking on tape.

"Why don't you think so?" Dee Dee asked me.

93

"Because I saw the way Adam looked at Janine," I said. "I know that look."

Dee Dee turned back to Adam. "Okay, so maybe you fell in love with her. What's that got to do with the videotape of Wordsworth and me talking?"

"Everything," Adam said.

Dee Dee scowled. "I don't know what you're talking about."

"I do," I said.

"Would you mind explaining it to me?" Dee Dee asked.

"Adam's willing to make a deal," I said. "He'll give us the tape, but in return, we have to give him Janine."

"*What?*" Dee Dee gasped again.

"You don't actually have to *give* her to me," Adam said. "You just have to get her to fall in love with me."

23

"Got any ideas?" Dee Dee asked. **We were sitting** together on a bench in Soundview Manor Park, watching the sailboats while we tried to figure out what to do.

"Suppose we get Janine to take us sailing," I said. "And we tell Adam to pretend he's drowning. Then Janine can save him and they'll fall in love."

"I don't think so," Dee Dee said. "Usually the person who gets saved falls in love with the person who saves them. We need it to be the other way around."

"Okay, suppose we get Adam to save Janine?"

"How?" Dee Dee asked. "Janine's a great swimmer."

"Then maybe he can save her from something else," I said.

"I don't know, Wordsworth, Janine's pretty darn good at just about everything she does." Dee Dee sounded thoroughly discouraged.

"I know!" I said. "We could get Janine to go skating on Mountain Drive and we could take the brake off her Rollerblades. Then Adam could catch her and save her from crashing."

"But if he misses she'll break her neck," said Dee Dee.

"Okay, then suppose we get Janine to test Roy's flying bicycle off the roof?" I asked. "And Adam could catch her."

"With what?" Dee Dee asked dismally. "A giant baseball mitt?"

"Good point," I admitted. "Okay, here's my last idea. Adam could find out what Janine loves to eat the most, and every day he feeds her some."

Dee Dee shook her head. "She's not a dog, Wordsworth. Maybe that worked with you, but it won't work on Janine." She stood up. "Come on, we might as well go home. We're not going to think of anything here."

We started to walk out of the park. I was getting worried.

"You're not going to give up?" I asked nervously. "I mean, you're not going to let him sell that tape to 'America's Stupidest Home Videos,' are you? You're not going to let them slice my brain into little slivers and put it under a microscope, are you?"

Wordsworth and the Tasty Treat Trick

"I'll try to come up with something, Wordsworth," Dee Dee said. "But I just don't know how."

This was starting to sound serious! How in the world could Dee Dee get Janine to fall in love with Adam? But if she didn't, then my nice, quiet, comfortable life with the Chandlers would be over forever. Who would guard their house? What would happen to Dee Dee if I wasn't there to look after her?

Dee Dee and I left the park and started to walk along the street toward our house. Neither of us said a word. I started to imagine what it would be like once my video appeared on "America's Stupidest Home Videos."

I'd become world famous!

I'd probably be on television constantly!

I might even get to be in movies!

Hey, that didn't sound so bad.

Unless those scientists got hold of me. I could see myself pinned to a large piece of plywood. *No! No! I'm too young to be dissected!*

"Hello down there!" a voice called, jarring me from my thoughts. Dee Dee and I looked up. Up in the sky, something that looked like a bicycle with huge wings flew over us.

Dee Dee cupped her hands around her mouth and shouted. "Is that you, Roy?"

"Yes!"

"Your invention works!" Dee Dee yelled.

"I'm afraid so!" Roy called back.

"Where are you going?"

"I don't know!" Roy shouted. "Dad forgot to add steering!"

A moment later he disappeared over the trees. Suddenly we heard the sound of rapid footsteps coming down the street. It was Leyland, running toward us with a video camera in his hands.

"Have you seen Roy?" he gasped, huffing and puffing.

"He went that way." Dee Dee pointed in the direction Roy had just gone.

"Right." Leyland dashed past us.

"I'm going to miss them when fame and fortune rip me from the warm cozy embrace of this quiet, mundane existence," I said with a sniff.

"Don't get maudlin, Wordsworth," Dee Dee said. "We're not giving up yet."

"You've got a plan?" I asked hopefully.

"No, but it doesn't mean I won't have one soon," she said.

We got back to the house and went into the kitchen. Janine was making herself a large glass of iced tea. She was wearing her tennis clothes and her face was flushed and outlined by damp streaks of hair. She'd obviously just come back from the courts.

"How was your game?" Dee Dee asked.

"Okay," Janine said. "So what did Adam want?"

"Oh, nothing important."

Janine took a gulp of iced tea and sat down at the kitchen table.

"Aren't you interested in what Adam thought of the dance last night?" Dee Dee asked.

"Not really," said Janine.

"You don't care what he thinks of you?" Dee Dee asked.

"Not particularly."

"How can you not care what someone thinks of you?" Dee Dee asked.

Condensation had collected on the outside of the glass of iced tea. Janine drew a face on it. "I don't know," she said. "Why should I? I mean, did Adam say something bad about me?"

"Oh, no!" Dee Dee gasped. "Nothing like that."

Janine shrugged. "So what's the point?"

Brrriiinggg! The phone rang.

"Would you get that?" Janine asked. "And if it's a boy, tell him I'm not here."

"What if it's Adam?" Dee Dee asked hopefully.

Janine gave her a funny look. "Is he a boy?"

"Yes."

"Then I'm not here."

Dee Dee answered the phone. "Hello? . . . Oh, uh, she's not here. . . . Okay, I'll tell her you called."

She hung up and sat down at the table again. "It was a guy."

Janine nodded and took another gulp of iced tea.

"I thought now that the dance is over they'd stop calling," Dee Dee said.

"No, now instead of twenty calls a day, it'll go back to three or four," Janine said.

"Why do you hate boys so much?" Dee Dee asked.

"I don't hate them," Janine said. "They're just boring. All they want to do is impress their friends."

"Suppose there was one you really did like," Dee Dee said.

"Okay."

"What would he be like?"

Janine sat back and swept a few long blond hairs off her face. "Let's see. First, he'd be taller than me. Then he'd be a really good athlete. And he'd have to like tennis and sailing and skiing. And be smart and good in school. But he wouldn't be a show-off. He'd be very modest. He wouldn't feel the need to impress people."

"But what if he had a fabulous personality?" Dee Dee asked.

"You're right," Janine said. "That could count for a lot."

"So what about Adam?" Dee Dee asked.

"Adam?" Janine's forehead wrinkled. "What about him?"

"Couldn't he qualify?"

"You mean, except for the fact that he's shorter than me, he's totally unathletic, he doesn't ski, sail, or play tennis, he doesn't seem particularly smart, and he tends to be a show-off?" Janine asked.

"What about his personality?" Dee Dee asked.

"What personality?" Janine replied.

Brrriiinggg! The phone rang again.

"Would you do the honors, please?" Janine asked.

"If it's a guy, you're not here?" Dee Dee said.

"You got it."

Dee Dee answered. It must have been a guy because she said Janine wasn't there. She hung up.

"I've got it!" Dee Dee said excitedly as she sat down. "You know how the boys stopped asking you to the dance once they found out you were going with Adam? Well, I know how you can make them stop calling forever!"

"How?"

"Just become Adam's girlfriend."

Janine finished her iced tea and put the glass in the sink. "It's an interesting idea, Dee Dee. But I have to tell you something. Given the choice between getting these annoying phone calls and having Adam Pickney as a boyfriend, I'll take the calls."

Then she walked out of the room.

24

"Catnip," I said. I was lying on Dee Dee's bed. It was late at night and the room was dark. The rest of the Chandlers were asleep, but Dee Dee and I were wide-awake.

"It doesn't work on humans," Dee Dee muttered.

"There must be something that does," I said.

"If there is, I don't know about it."

"I don't want them to take away my brain and slice it into little pieces," I whimpered.

Dee Dee put her arm around my neck and kissed me on my head. "Be brave, Wordsworth."

"That's easy for you to say." I sniffed. "No one's going to put *your* brain under a microscope."

"And they won't put yours under one either," Dee Dee said, hugging me. "If Adam sells that video to 'America's Stupidest Home Videos,' we'll run away."

Wordsworth and the Tasty Treat Trick

"If Adam sells that video, the whole country will know about me," I groaned. "I don't think we'll get very far without being spotted."

"Then I'll disguise you," Dee Dee said.

"As what?"

"We could paint you brown and pretend you were a dachshund," she said.

"Except I'd be the world's biggest dachshund. They're puny little things, and they don't have these long, handsome ears."

"Dad could make you short stilts and you could pretend you were a beagle," Dee Dee said.

I lifted my head and stared at her in the dark. "If you're going *that* far, why not just dress me up as a small man with a fake beard? Why not—"

"Wait!" Dee Dee gasped.

"What?"

"I just got an idea! If Adam tricked us, why can't we trick him?"

25

The next day, Dee Dee drew up a flyer and had three copies made at the copy shop in town. The flyer said:

GET RICH AND FAMOUS!

"America's Stupidest Home Videos" is coming to Soundview Manor. Dig out or make your stupidest videos and bring them to room 203 at the Yacht Club on Wednesday between 10:00 A.M. and 2:00 P.M. Don't hesitate! This could be your chance to get really rich!

"It's a nice flyer," I said as we walked home from the copy shop. "But why did you only make three copies?"

"Because I only want Adam to see it," Dee Dee said.

At Adam's house, she stapled one flyer to a telephone pole near the sidewalk and another to his fence. She folded the third one and slid it into the newspaper lying on the walk.

"There," she said. "He's bound to see one of them."

"Great," I said. "Now why don't we go home so I can have a nap." I was tired. I hadn't slept well the night before because I'd had bad dreams about scientists in white jackets chasing me with sharp scalpels.

"No way," Dee Dee said. "First we have to plead for mercy with Adam."

"Why?" I asked.

"Because we have to make it look like we really tried to get Janine to be his girlfriend."

"Why?"

"Because otherwise it won't be realistic." Dee Dee headed up the walk to Adam's house. She rang the doorbell and waited, but no one answered.

"Looks like he isn't home," I said.

"Yes, he is," said Dee Dee. "Listen."

I listened, and heard the faint sounds of music coming from inside the house.

"He's in there, but he doesn't hear us." Dee Dee knocked loudly on the door. "Adam? Hello!"

Finally Adam came to the door. Dee Dee and I were shocked by his appearance. His hair was spiky, his clothes were all black, and he was wearing the earrings and nose ring again.

"What do you want?" he asked in an unfriendly tone.

"We need to talk to you," Dee Dee said.

"About what?"

"Janine."

Adam shook his head. "There's nothing to talk about. Either you got her to be my girlfriend or you didn't."

"I tried, Adam," Dee Dee said, trying to sound desperate. "I really, really did."

"Yeah, right." Adam smirked. He acted like he didn't believe her.

"But it's true!" Dee Dee insisted. "I talked to her. I tried to convince her. I really tried."

"Sorry, but trying doesn't count." Adam started to close the front door.

"Wait!" Dee Dee gasped.

"Now what?" Adam asked impatiently.

"How can you expect her to fall in love with you when you're wearing those clothes . . . and that nose ring?"

"What do you mean?" Adam asked. "These are cool clothes."

"Not to Janine."

"Well, tough." Once again Adam started to close the door.

Dee Dee grabbed it and held it open. "What are you going to do?"

"I'm gonna make a ton of money on the video, and then I'm gonna mend my broken heart by going on the biggest shopping spree anyone ever saw."

Bang! He slammed the door shut.

Dee Dee looked down at me and winked. "Okay, Wordsworth, now we have to see if he takes the bait."

We went back down the walk and toward our house. Roy was sitting on the front steps with his head in his hands and a forlorn look on his face.

"Hi, Roy," Dee Dee said.

"Hi," he said, moping.

"What's wrong?"

"I don't have a video for 'America's Stupidest Home Videos.'"

"Your flying bicycle looked great," Dee Dee said.

"It didn't crash," Roy said. "I made a perfect landing behind the middle school. Dad even got it on video."

"Isn't there a show for smart videos?" Dee Dee asked.

"Get real. No one wants to see other people succeed. They want to see failures. It makes them feel good to see that there's someone who's even dumber than they are. I just wish I could come up with something really dumb."

"Maybe you could use one of Dad's old inventions," Dee Dee suggested.

"Naw, none of them work," Roy said. "The only thing that works these days is the riding vacuum cleaner."

"Maybe you could use that."

"But it works," Roy said. "I keep telling you, Dee Dee, things aren't funny when they work. They're only funny when they don't work."

"Well, maybe the riding vacuum works inside, but what about outside?" Dee Dee asked.

Roy suddenly sat up straight. "That's it! I'll make a video showing how the riding vacuum works inside, then I'll ride it outside. I could ride it straight through the park, over the rocks, up the ramp, and into Bell Island Sound! They'd *love* that!"

"But won't that ruin Dad's invention?" Dee Dee asked.

"He's building a new one," Roy said. "I don't think he'll care if I use the old one. What a great idea! Thanks, Dee Dee."

Roy jumped up and ran inside. Dee Dee turned to me and sighed. "Why can't our problems be that easy to solve?"

26

The next morning everyone slept late as usual. Dee Dee was the first to come down to the kitchen. She was lugging a large white shopping bag.

"What's that?" I asked with a yawn.

"Our disguise."

"Disguise for what?" I asked.

"We're playing the trick on Adam, remember?"

"With a disguise?" I asked. "May I remind you that I'm a seventy-five-pound basset hound. What are you going to disguise me as? A giant walking salami?"

"You'll see." Dee Dee smiled. She looked very confident. I always worry when people look confident.

"Why are you acting so self-assured?" I asked. "Adam's not stupid. He knows that video is worth a fortune. He's not going to trade it for some old Marvel cards."

"Who said that?" Janine asked, walking into the kitchen and catching us by surprise.

"Who said what?" Dee Dee asked innocently.

"Someone just said something about Marvel cards," Janine said, looking around. "It was a male voice. Where is he?"

"Where's who?" Dee Dee asked.

"The person who was talking about Marvel cards."

"What about them?" Roy asked as he entered the kitchen.

"Were you just talking about them?" Janine asked.

"No," said Roy.

"Well, *someone* was," Janine said. "And I'd like to know who it was."

"Let me know when you find out," Roy said. "I've got a ton of them. So guess what?"

"What?" Dee Dee asked.

"Dad said he'd let me ride the old vacuum cleaner into Bell Island Sound."

"Why?" Janine asked.

"Because it'll make a great video," said Roy.

Janine rolled her eyes. "Is it my imagination, or has this whole family gone lame?"

Dee Dee looked at the kitchen clock. It was 9:30. She pushed back her chair and picked up the bag.

Wordsworth and the Tasty Treat Trick

"Time to go. Come on Wordsworth, let's take a walk."

"What's in the bag?" Janine asked.

"Uh . . ." Dee Dee looked stumped for a second. "A disguise."

"Why?" Janine asked.

"Why not?" Dee Dee replied with a grin. Then she led me out of the kitchen. Outside on the sidewalk, I asked her where we were going.

"The yacht club," she said. "Remember those phony flyers we put up around Adam's house?"

"But Adam's not going to give us the video just because of that flyer," I said.

"Of course not," Dee Dee said. "That's why I brought the disguise."

"Why am I getting a bad feeling about this?" I asked woefully.

"Hush, we're getting close."

We turned up the driveway of the yacht club. Unlike the last time, when we went in the dark, this time the sun was shining.

"We can't just walk in," I said in a low voice. "Someone's going to see us."

"Shush. Just act normal."

"I *am* acting normal. But normally I'm a dog, and dogs aren't allowed here."

"Duck!" Dee Dee suddenly whispered.

27

The next thing I knew, Dee Dee yanked me into the hedge lining the driveway and crouched down.

"Where?" I asked.

"Where what?" Dee Dee whispered.

"Where's the duck? And why are we hiding from it?"

"No, silly, I wanted *you* to duck."

"Me? I'm a basset hound. If I get any closer to the ground, I'll be under it."

"Shh! The guard." Dee Dee pointed at the club entrance.

She was right. The guard in the dark green uniform had just pushed open the front door and come outside. We watched as he started around the side of the yacht club.

"Come on," Dee Dee whispered. Still crouching,

she scurried quietly along the hedge, carrying the shopping bag. "Stay low."

"Very funny," I muttered.

Dee Dee looked back at me and grinned sheepishly. We snuck in through the front door and quickly went up the old stairway to the left. A moment later we got into the room where we'd watched the dance. Inside was the desk and the chair with the tall back. Dee Dee reached into the shopping bag and took out a small pillow, one of Leyland's old topcoats, a hat, and sunglasses.

"What is this?" I asked.

"You'll see." Dee Dee took out Janine's makeup kit.

"Does Janine know you took that?" I asked.

"I didn't *take* it. I only *borrowed* it."

"Somehow I don't think Janine is going to appreciate that difference," I said.

"Let me worry about that." Dee Dee opened the kit and took out something that resembled a thick pencil. Staring into the mirror, she drew a dark line above her upper lip.

"What's that?" I asked.

"A mustache," she said.

"I never would have guessed."

"I wish you wouldn't be so negative, Wordsworth," she said. "I'm doing this all for you. You *could* show a little appreciation."

"Just give me one lamb chop and I'll show you all the appreciation in the world," I said.

"I don't know how you can be thinking about food at a time like this."

"I can think about food at *any* time."

Dee Dee looked at her watch. "Uh-oh, it's five of ten. We better get ready. Wordsworth, you have to get into the chair."

"Why?"

"Because you're going to do all the talking."

"*What?*"

"You've got the deep voice," she said. "If I talk, he'll know I'm a girl."

"Then what *are* you going to do?" I asked.

"I'm going to sit on you and smoke a cigar."

I stared at her in disbelief. "I'm starting to think Janine is right. You *have* gone lame!"

"If you can come up with a better plan, I'm all ears," she said.

"No, I'm the one with the ears."

Dee Dee groaned. "You know what I meant."

28

"Ow!" I grumbled.

"Stop wiggling so much!" Dee Dee hissed. She was sitting on me. I hadn't been able to think of a better plan.

"It hurts!" I complained. "You're not so light anymore. You're putting a terrible strain on my back."

"It's only for a little while." Dee Dee pulled on Leyland's coat. It covered me, too, but I was able to see through a buttonhole. She'd also put on the hat and sunglasses. "I have to sit on your back or I won't look tall enough."

"This is ridiculous," I muttered.

"Hush! Now remember that you have to do all the talking," she said. "You've got to make Adam believe that you're a real TV producer from Hollywood."

"How do I do that?" I asked.

"You act impatient and obnoxious," Dee Dee said. "And use words like 'kiddo,' and 'baby,' and 'sweetheart.'"

"That's it?"

"Tell him that you're going to consider his video. If it's as good as he says it is, he'll undoubtedly win the weekly prize of twenty thousand dollars and become eligible for the grand prize of two hundred thousand dollars."

"*He could get that much?*" I was shocked.

"Uh-huh."

"We could buy a lot of lamb chops with that," I said. "Why don't we forget about Adam and make our own video?"

"The scientists will want your brain, remember?"

"Oh, yeah."

Rap! Rap! Someone knocked on the door.

"Tell him just a minute," Dee Dee whispered.

"Uh, just a minute, kiddo," I said.

I heard her strike a match and soon smelled yucky cigar smoke. Dee Dee started to cough.

"This is awful!" She gasped and wheezed. A cloud of cigar smoke hung in the air around us.

"Are you sure it's necessary?" I asked.

"Yes," Dee Dee said. "All those Hollywood producers smoke cigars. I saw it on a TV show. Besides, the smoke will make it harder for Adam to see us. You can tell him to come in now."

"Okay, come in, sweetheart," I said.

The door opened and Adam stuck his head in and looked around nervously. "Is this the place for 'America's Stupidest Home Videos'?"

"You got it, baby," I said. "What's up?"

Adam stepped into the room. "Well, I have this video."

"Congratulations, kiddo," I said. "So do about a hundred million other people. Look, I'm a busy dog—"

Ow! Under the coat, Dee Dee kicked me.

"Uh . . . er, I meant, I'm working like a dog," I said. "I'm a busy man. Make your pitch and get out. Don't waste my time, sweetheart."

"Oh, believe me, I won't," Adam said. "Once you see this tape, you'll freak."

"I'll freak? Forget it, babysweets, I freaked a long time ago. What's your name, sweetheart?"

"Adam Pickney."

"Well listen, Adam Pickney baby, it takes a lot to make me freak, you understand? This is gonna have to be one boffo video, my friend."

"Believe me, it is. You're not going to believe this, but this is a video of a talking dog," Adam said, holding up the tape.

"What do you mean, a talking dog?" I said. "There's no such thing. Get outta here, you dirtbag scuzzball, you're wasting my time."

"No, you gotta believe me," Adam begged. "This dog actually talks. You put this tape on your show and the whole world's gonna flip out."

"What is it, some kind of a trick?" I asked.

"No, sir, it's for real," Adam said. "You could probably put the dog himself on TV."

"Adam, sweetheart, baby, tell me something," I said. "You know this dog?"

"Yeah, he lives with my next-door neighbors," Adam said. "His name's Wordsworth and he's a fat old basset hound."

"What do you mean, fat?" I said. "He's lost weight," *Ow!* Dee Dee kicked me under the coat.

"What?" Adam scowled.

"I said, Adam, babycakes, I can't *wait* to see your video."

Adam hesitated. "Well, I figured maybe you'd pay me for it."

"Pay you?" I acted shocked. "Why you two-bit dweeb sleezeball punk. This is 'America's Stupidest Home Videos.' We're one of the most successful shows on TV! We don't pay anybody for their videos."

"But you've never had a tape like this," Adam argued.

Wordsworth and the Tasty Treat Trick

"Oh yeah? You think your tape is so great? Well, let me tell you something, Adam Picknose. If this tape is everything you say it is, you'll win our weekly twenty-thousand-dollar prize and be eligible for the grand prize of two hundred thousand dollars. And let me tell you something else, if you really got a talking dog on there, I can just about promise you that you will win the grand prize."

"You think?" Adam asked eagerly.

"What do you mean, do I think? I'm the one who decides these things, you bonehead! Now give me that tape."

Adam hesitated again. "You mean, I'm just supposed to give it to you? Just like that?"

"Hey, you want your video to be on TV, right?"

"Well, er, sure."

"So, tell me something, baby brainwad, how do you expect it to get on TV if you don't give it to me, huh?"

"Well, er, couldn't you sign for it or something?" Adam asked. "Like couldn't we have some kind of contract? Because this is my only copy of the tape."

"Adam, sweetheart, babykins, honey lamb, I'm disappointed in you." I pretended to be hurt. "Is it my imagination or are you saying you don't trust me? 'Cause if you're saying you don't trust me, then we can end this meeting right now. You can walk out of here and we'll forget the whole thing. You can go home and talk to your dog, and I'll go back to California and still be the producer of one of the most successful TV shows in the world. Let's get something straight, pea-brain, I don't need you, *you* need me!"

"I didn't mean to insult you, Mister . . . uh, Mister—"

"Mr. Big," I said.

"Don't get me wrong, Mr. Big," Adam said. "I really, really do want my video to be on your show."

"Then what's the problem, lovelump?" I asked. "You think I'm gonna steal your tape? You think I made it this far in the entertainment business by stealing tapes from dirtbag geeks like you? Let me tell you something, you amoeba, it took years of hard work to get to this point. I struggled, I suffered, I worked my paws to the bone—"

Dee Dee kicked me again.

"Hey, cut it out!" I snapped.

Adam frowned. "Cut what out?"

"Uh, cut out the confusion clause," I said. "Now let's get down to business, talk turkey, cut a deal, take a meeting, do lunch, gross points on the back end, pay or play, what do you say?"

"Well, as long as you promise that I'll get what I deserve," Adam said.

"Oh, Adam, baby, sweetheart, lover boy, believe me, you'll get what you deserve."

Adam stepped forward and put the tape on the desk. Just then the door on the other side of the room swung open. Someone said, "Hey, what's going on in here?"

29

It was the guard!

"Hey! You can't just barge in here!" I yelled. "We're in the middle of serious negotiations. Call my secretary. Make an appointment. I think I have an opening in the year 2010."

"What are you talking about?" the guard asked. "You're not supposed to be in here."

"Yeah, he is," said Adam. "He's Mr. Big from 'America's Stupidest Home Videos.' They're using this room today as an office."

"No, he's not," the guard said. "I don't know anything about any Mr. Big using any room here. The club doesn't allow that kind of thing."

"It doesn't?" Adam turned and stared at Dee Dee and me. "Then who . . . ?"

His eyes went to the tape lying on the desk.

"Get it, Wordsworth!" Dee Dee shouted.

I jumped out from inside the coat and landed on the desk. Adam and I lunged for the tape at the same second.

Bonk! Our heads banged into each other.

Ouch! I managed to get my jaws around the tape and jump down from the table.

"Come back here!" Adam shouted.

I raced around the table with Adam right behind me.

Dee Dee waited until I passed and then stuck her leg out.

"Oooof!"

Crash! Adam tripped over Dee Dee's leg and went flying.

"Run, Wordsworth!" Dee Dee yelled.

I headed for the door.

"You again!" the guard shouted, and tried to block my path. I dodged left, but he moved that way. I dodged right, and he moved to stop me again. I threw a head fake and ran straight through his legs!

Whomp! The guard fell over backward.

"Go! Wordsworth, go!" Dee Dee shouted, and ran out of the room behind me.

"You're dead meat!" Adam screamed, and chased after us.

"Come back here!" yelled the guard, following him.

Wordsworth and the Tasty Treat Trick

I bounded down the stairs and out the front doors of the club with the tape still in my mouth.

"To the park!" Dee Dee shouted behind me.

Right! Of course! I headed for the park.

"I'll kill you!" Adam yelled, chasing us.

"Come back here!" shouted the club guard.

A green van was coming down the street toward us. On the sides in big bright orange letters were the words AMERICA'S STUPIDEST HOME VIDEOS. As we all raced toward it, a man with short brown hair and a tan safari jacket jumped out.

"Hey, what's going on?" he asked.

I couldn't stop, and raced past him with Dee Dee following and Adam and the guard behind her.

"Hey, Jim!" the man from the van yelled. "Get the camera!"

A few moments later three more people joined the chase. Now I was being followed by Dee Dee, Adam, the club guard, and the film crew from ASHV!

30

I shot through the park, crossed the paths, and scrambled around the benches and trees.

"Toward the water, Wordsworth!" Dee Dee shouted.

Ah! So that's what she wanted me to do!

"Gimme back my tape!" Adam screamed.

"Come back here!" yelled the club guard.

"Are you getting this?" the director shouted to his film crew.

Ahead I could see the rocks leading toward the water. Oh, no! There was Roy on the Chandler E-Z Glide Self-Propelled Riding Vacuum Cleaner! There was Leyland filming him!

I ran past Roy.

"Hey, Wordsworth!" he shouted. "Where're you—"

Ker-splash! I hit the water!

Wordsworth and the Tasty Treat Trick

Ker-splash! Dee Dee dove in behind me. "Swim out deep, Wordsworth!" she shouted. "Don't drop the tape until you're really deep!"

Ker-splash! Adam dove in behind us. "I'll kill you, you no-good mutt!"

Ker-splash! The club guard jumped in. "Come back here!"

Ker-splash! Roy drove the riding vacuum cleaner into the sound.

The film crew from ASHV stopped at the edge of the water.

"Are you getting this?" the director shouted. "Promise me you're getting this!"

I dogpaddled toward the deep water.

"Keep swimming, Wordsworth!" Dee Dee yelled as she splashed behind me.

I swam as fast as I could. Unfortunately, basset hounds are not known for their record speeds in aquatic events.

"Drop that tape and you're dead!" Adam screamed as he swam. "You hear me, Wordsworth? Dead!"

I kept swimming. Adam was catching up to Dee Dee.

"Keep swimming, Wordsworth!" Dee Dee shouted. "I'll stop Adam." She turned and started to splash water in Adam's face. Adam reached out, put his hand on her head, and pushed her under!

Wordsworth and the Tasty Treat Trick

"Hey!" Roy shouted as he splashed toward them. "Are you trying to drown my sister?"

Glub! Dee Dee came back up to the surface and gasped for breath. Meanwhile Adam was splashing toward me again.

"Go, Wordsworth!" Dee Dee shouted. "I'm okay! Go!"

I started swimming again. I knew the water underneath me was pretty deep, but it would soon get deeper.

"I'll get you!" Adam was splashing and thrashing closer and closer. "I swear I'll kill you!"

I was dogpaddling for dear life. Adam's splashing was getting closer and closer.

Suddenly I felt him grab my tail!

The next thing I knew, he pulled me under!

31

I was struggling with Adam under the water, but I was tired and my lungs were burning for air.

Then everything went black.

The next thing I remember, someone's arm was across my chest and I was being pulled through the water.

"Over here!" someone shouted. "That's it! Just a little farther!"

Hands reached down and pulled me out of the water. I felt myself being hauled over the gunwale of a boat and lowered to the floor.

"Oh, Wordsworth, you're okay!" I recognized Dee Dee's voice and felt her arms go around my neck. She hugged me and pressed her lips close to my ear.

"*You did it!*" she whispered. "*The tape sank!*"

I opened my eyes and saw men in blue uniforms

standing around us. It was the harbor police! They were pulling Roy and Adam into the boat.

"Did you see him?" Roy sputtered, and pointed a dripping finger at Adam. "He tried to drown my sister and her dog!"

"No, I didn't!" Adam shouted.

"Yes, you did," one of the policemen said. "I saw you, too."

He spun Adam around and clipped his wrists together with handcuffs.

"But I wasn't," Adam insisted.

"Then what were you doing?" one of the harbor police asked.

"They stole a videotape," Adam said. "I was just trying to get it back."

"A videotape of what?" one of the men asked.

"Uh . . . uh . . ." Adam glared at me, tongue-tied.

Groof! Groof! I barked, and wagged my tail like some kind of dumb dog.

"What videotape?" the harbor policeman asked again.

Adam just shook his head. "Forget it, you'd never believe me."

32

⁂

Several months later some of the Chandlers gathered in the den around the family's only TV set. On the screen was a fuzzy commercial about breakfast cereal.

"Geez, Dad, when are we gonna get a new TV?" Janine asked. "Everyone else has one."

"Just because other people have something doesn't mean we have to," Leyland said as he adjusted the rabbit ears.

"It would be sort of interesting to see this in color," Janine said.

"Quiet, everyone, the show's coming back on!" Dee Dee said.

The music for "America's Stupidest Home Videos" came on, along with the host, a handsome dark-haired man in a dark suit.

"All right!" the host announced. "And now it's

time to announce this week's winner of the twenty-thousand-dollar prize for the stupidest home video. Will it be the world's largest collection of toilet bowls? Or the man who drinks milkshakes through his nose? Or riding vacuum cleaner chases guard chasing boy chasing girl chasing dog? And the winner is . . . *Riding vacuum cleaner chases guard chasing boy chasing girl chasing dog!*"

"Ya-hoo!" Janine and Dee Dee jumped to their feet and cheered. On the screen was the video of Roy on the riding vacuum following the yacht-club guard following Adam following Dee Dee following me into Bell Island Sound.

Next, the picture shifted to Roy and Flora standing in the ASHV audience as the host joined them.

"So, how did this all happen?" he asked, holding the microphone in front of Roy.

"Well, it basically happened because our next-door neighbor thinks our dog can talk," Roy said.

The host of ASHV raised his eyebrows and turned to the camera. "Did you hear *that*? He thought their dog could *talk*! Now *that* would be a *great video*!"

In the den, Dee Dee turned to me and winked.

"Ahem." Someone cleared their throat.

We turned to see that Janine was studying us. "Adam's wrong, right? Wordsworth can't really talk, can he?"

133

Groof! I barked.

"No way," Dee Dee said, putting one hand behind her back.

"You sure?"

"Absolutely."

Janine nodded and looked back at the TV. It was a good thing that she didn't see Dee Dee crossing her fingers.

Todd Strasser has written many award-winning novels for young and teenage readers. He speaks frequently at schools about the craft of writing and conducts writing workshops for young people. He lives with his wife, children, and dog in a place near the water.

MONSTERKIDS

LOOK FOR THESE SPOOKY MONSTERKIDS STORIES BY GERTRUDE GRUESOME:

Drak's Slumber Party
Life isn't easy for a third-grader monster. Drak's just trying to fit in. That's why his slumber party has to be the best. But Drak's blood-sucking cousins have just arrived! Can he save his friends *and* the party?

Frank's Field Trip
Frank N. Stein has monster-sized problems. He can't seem to get a break—except when he's breaking things. His class is at the museum and about to lose the science competition. Everyone is counting on Frank to save the day!

Harry Goes to Camp
How will Harry Wolf survive a month of summer camp? Whenever there's a full moon, he needs to do what all werewolves do: eat raw hamburgers and howl at the moon. For Harry and his best friend Alec, will their first summer at sleepaway camp be a total disaster?

Boris Bigfoot's Big Feat
He's the new kid in school, and he doesn't fit in. But when Boris Bigfoot starts kicking a soccer ball around, the coach sees his new star player. Before long, Boris not only fits in, he's the hero of the team.

The Curse of Cleo Patrick's Mummy*
According to ancient mummy legend grave misfortune will fall on anyone who dares to steal from a mummy. Cleo Patrick's mother can't find her favorite bracelet. Cleo and her friends play dress-up with her mom's jewelry, but they didn't steal anything. So why is everything going wrong?

Zelda's Zombie Dance*
Zelda LaMort has trouble making friends—it's hard to fit in when you're dead.

*coming soon